FROST MATE

A DEMONS OF FROSTERIA NOVELLA

ELLE BEAUMONT
CANDACE ROBINSON

Midnight Tide
PUBLISHING

Frost Mate

Copyright © 2021 by Elle Beaumont & Candace Robinson

Published by Midnight Tide Publishing
www.midnighttidepublishing.com

Cover design by Danielle Doolittle | DoElle Designs |
www.doelledesigns.wix.com

For those who believe their soul has a mate out there

KORRETH

Snow fell from the cerulean sky, dusting Korreth's eyelashes before it melted into trails of water down his face. A snowstorm was on its way and a fresh blanket of white would soon cover the landscape again. The wind was picking up, and when one had grown up in Frosteria, they noticed the shifts in weather.

There was a crispness to the air that nipped at Korreth's nose, telling him it would only get worse. That the true winter in the kingdom would soon settle over them.

He was a warrior and wouldn't duck inside the barracks to wait out the storm. Instead, he watched impassively as two young warriors sparred and kicked up chunks of ice. This was what they had been born for, and why the frost demon king, Morozko, used a drop of his blood in the snow to create the krampi. *His sons and daughters*, as he called them. Morozko's Immortal Army.

Korreth assessed each warrior's movements, their timing, and how they could improve. A well-connected elbow to the smaller male's jaw sent him to the ground. He spat out blood, growled low, and sprang to his feet once again.

A cacophony of shouts rang out as the larger of the two males warred to shove his comrade out of the ring. Several krampi standing by cheered, while others cursed and begged for the other to push back.

The bigger male with red, curly hair ducked low, sweep-kicking the lesser warrior off balance. With a thud, the smaller male hit the ground hard.

The loser slammed his fist on the ground, howling in dismay. "You son of a—"

"Captain Korreth," a deep voice called from behind, silencing everyone in the vicinity. The rustling of fabric echoed off the ice as the krampi bowed to the newcomer.

When Korreth twisted around to face the commanding voice, he bowed at the waist, pounding a fist to his chest. "Major Enox." His eyes assessed the other, noting the tense lines of the male's face. Major Enox was shorter than Korreth, but had a thicker build and exuded dominance. The tension rippling from him only added to his often-oppressive aura.

"At ease," Enox bit out. He motioned to Korreth, who cast a fleeting glance in his subordinate's direction.

"Continue with the training," Korreth ordered, then followed Enox as he walked down the ice path that led away from the barracks. Before them loomed the Frosteria Mountains, unforgiving, even to the strongest krampi.

Korreth frowned. *Had something new developed with the changelings?* It hadn't been long since their last attack on one of the lesser villages in Frosteria. Had they struck again?

While most changelings lived on the other side of the

mountains, a different group inhabited the base of the range near the krampi villages. No matter how hard the warriors tried to eradicate them, the changelings always survived.

"Word just came in from the outlying villages. The changelings grow bolder, more violent, and we need more recruits." Enox propped his elbow on his other arm and leaned his cleft chin on a fist. Sighing, he looked skyward. "We're desperate enough to take anyone." Frustration wrinkled his forehead and when he moved his hand, he ran his fingers along the tanned skin to smooth out the lines.

Korreth knew the tension grew with each passing day, but were they so desperate that they needed to pick anyone for their army? All krampi were strong, possessed a unique magic even, but not everyone was cut out to be a part of Morozko's Immortal Army.

"Sir, with all due—"

"Korreth, the changelings grow bolder in the human world too. New trainees will arrive any moment. It won't just be up to you—the other superior warriors will be training them as well. Understand?"

Korreth's eyebrows lifted. A thousand questions tumbled in his mind, one of which was, *what the fuck is actually going on?* But he couldn't bring himself to speak against the major in such a way. Still, instinct screamed at him, warning him not to take this lightly.

And he wouldn't.

"Understood, sir." He bowed once more, thumping his fist against his chest. "I will do whatever I can." Korreth flexed his fingers by his side, but otherwise remained inscrutable. Already he was training new recruits. To add to his load—to his comrades—would only burden them further. Warriors needed time to train, but with the steady push from the major, Korreth would not get that time.

"As you were then, Captain. I trust your guidance with the warriors." Enox inclined his head, then walked away.

Korreth wasn't sure which was more worrisome, the fact the changelings' activity was on the rise, or that the army needed recruits so desperately with the war against the lesser demons.

Korreth's lip curled at the thought.

"Captain," a feminine voice called out. "There is a brawl…"

Of course there is. He ran his knuckles under his chin, subduing the mounting annoyance, for now. "Tell me it isn't the fools from the spar?"

Sila's white hair whipped across her face as a strong wind blew by. Her dark eyes never wavered from his. "Sir, it is them."

"Why am I not surprised?" He tilted his head back, catching more snowflakes against his face, and watched as the wind swept through them, creating small, dizzying cyclones. A lock of his wavy hair sprung loose from behind his horns and tickled above his brows. "Deal with the brawlers, knock them out if you have to." He lowered his head, narrowing his eyes. "I don't have the time to deal with their pettiness."

"And there are new recruits." Her tone went up an octave, but as Korreth met her probing gaze, she glanced downward to avoid eye contact.

Korreth *really* didn't have the time to deal with the fools now that the trainees had arrived. "If they don't listen, you have my permission to blast them with your magic." He jammed his forefinger and thumb into his mouth, then produced a shrill whistle that struck the air.

Nothing happened at first. But a moment later, the distinct sound of pounding hooves striking the icy ground sounded. As the creature rounded the bend, its massive ivory rack glimmered in the gray lighting. Instead of antlers similar to a moose, the creature boasted ones that looked much like barbed wire. The main bony-structure jutted outward from its skull, and nodules twisted around, sticking this way and that. Sturdy legs supported a thick steel-gray muscular frame, and the reindeer's red eyes glowed like crimson flames.

Dral, Korreth's familiar and companion.

While it was common that krampi had a bonded familiar, not all had one, but when they did, it was a connection that went beyond magic and deep into the soul for them both.

Upon creation, Morozko gifted his sons and daughters unique magic that would develop in their later years. For Korreth, he could fashion weapons from ice. All he needed was water. Other krampi could transform ice into beasts or call on snowstorms. It seemed as though Frosteria had known the road Korreth's life would take him down.

As the beast halted in front of him, Korreth grabbed a hold of the saddle's leather horn and pulled himself up, then urged his familiar down the icy road. Behind them, a cloud of fine snow kicked up in their wake.

In a matter of minutes, Korreth approached the drop off point, where a cluster of krampi awaited him, restless and tense. He scanned their faces, a few of them were familiar, but one stood out amongst the rest. While most shoved at each other, a female lingered off to the side, arms folded and her dark brown eyes locked on Korreth.

Long, thick locks of blonde hair hung freely down her back, but it wasn't her hair, nor her eyes, that made Korreth's heart thump. Her leather pants clung to her curves and filled him with the desire to hoist her onto his hips. And her full, rosy lips begged him to taste and nip them. It was like a punch to the gut.

Korreth sucked in a breath, shoving the inexplicable tightening of his chest away. In a beat, he composed himself again. "Welcome, Children of Morozko. I am Captain Korreth and you will address me as Captain, only. You've either been drafted or joined willingly. Either way, I don't care." His cool words brought a bark of laughter from a gaggle of krampi, but Korreth didn't so much as crack a smile.

"We have a job to do, which is to subdue and eventually eradicate the changelings. Time is of the essence, and I will push you beyond your limits. If you don't believe yourself capable, bow out now."

When no one budged, Korreth nodded. "Very well, follow me."

"Wait," a feminine voice cut through the murmurs. "I have a question."

Halfway turning his mount around, Korreth paused and twisted in the saddle. His gaze homed in on the blonde who had caught his attention before. The wind flipped her hair over her horns, but she didn't fuss with them. She just stood there, staring at him. "I don't recall asking if anyone had questions."

As if he hadn't said anything at all, she continued, "When do we get to kill the changelings?"

Torn between annoyance and surprise, Korreth's lips twitched in the faintest of smirks. "Sooner than you think, that is, if you aren't killed first."

2

ZIRA

A WINTRY WONDERLAND DIDN'T MAKE ZIRA'S WORLD A paradise. Not even close.

There had been three reasons she'd volunteered to be a part of Morozko's Immortal Army.

One—her family. Two—her lover. Three—her friend. All dead.

They had been ripped apart, their limbs dismembered, and their lungs torn out and eaten. Yet their hearts had been left behind, displayed in their ripped-open rib cages. Zira would have met the same fate if she hadn't been out hunting in the forest. Sometimes, she wished she would have died in her village with her loved ones, but the larger part desperately ached for revenge.

Since that cruel day, a year ago, her thoughts were focused on one thing. Finding a way to destroy every living changeling in Frosteria. But Zira was only a lone female. She was exceptional with a bow and held a bit of magic to create small things from snow and water, however, she was not stealthy enough to slip into the changelings' territory beyond the mountainous barrier. She had believed the time would one day come. And that one day had finally arrived. Perhaps not in the way she'd planned, but still a way to destroy the wicked creatures.

When Morozko's warriors had come into her village to recruit new krampi to their army, Zira was the first to volunteer. Over the years, the changelings continued to invade villages throughout Frosteria, destroying, taking, eating. Her village remained broken from the changelings' attack. After her family's slaughter, Zira couldn't sleep inside her home any longer—she'd taken to the forest instead.

The warriors hadn't allowed the recruits to mount their stags, instead they'd been forced to walk the entire ice trail back to the center of Frosteria where Morozko's warriors dwelled. On the long trek through the biting cold, with heavy gusts of winds, not once had they been given a break, only when night fell and it was time to sleep. It was a teaching method. In a war, a battle, one didn't have the leisure to relieve themselves when they wished.

As Zira now stood in a crowd of new recruits, focused on the male in front of her, the captain, she could tell he was a stiff with his severe expression. But he was a damn sexy one. He wore tight dark pants tucked into his boots, and his uniform top, which buttoned up, was crimson and black. The sleeves of it were rolled up and the collar flicked upward. His horns curled toward the sky, by far some of the longest she'd ever seen—a sign every female krampi knew meant he was well-endowed. A heat spread through her as she studied the hard line of his square jaw, the way the wind tousled his rugged curls, the tilt of his plump lips.

After the long journey, her legs ached, her muscles sore.

Even her fucking horns were tired. But she didn't show it—she wouldn't show any weaknesses in front of this male.

Another male pushed forward through the crowd, dressed in a uniform matching the captain's. Where had he come from? The barracks? She'd been too focused on Captain Korreth. The new male was tall, broad, with dark hair cascading down to his waist. His horns were almost as long as the captain's. The male's sharp green gaze pierced each individual in the snow.

"You may call me Major Enox." He struck his chest with his fist, the sound echoing. "You think you are to have a break after coming here? Not today. I'm assigning you into pairs with a warrior now. I've gotten recent word of a stirring within the mortal world, and it could become catastrophic if not snuffed out soon. You have one week to train and prepare yourselves."

Zira peered at the captain who sat rigidly atop his beastly reindeer. A line creased his brow while he studied the major, as though he hadn't been expecting this turn of events. Korreth's beast kicked at the snow, seeming to prepare itself for what was to come. The creature was unlike any reindeer she'd ever seen—glowing red eyes, fur the sleekest of gray covering its massive body. Its twisted antlers protruded from its forehead, sharper than any stag's, with spikes like thorns running up their length.

The major lifted his chin and ventured through the crowd, assigning one recruit at a time to a frost warrior. Zira scanned the warriors, wondering who she would be paired with. She didn't truly care as long as they would get her one step closer to the changelings.

"You." The major pointed at Zira and she jerked her head

up. "It's your lucky day—you're assigned with Captain Korreth."

Zira's brows slid up her forehead and she met the ice-blue gaze of the captain. He studied her in what might have been annoyance, as though he found her to be the weakest link in the crowd of recruits. However, this was the perfect opportunity for her—she would be trained by the best... and the sexiest.

Korreth's beast walked toward her and turned to the side. The captain peered down at Zira, scanning her from head to toe, then slowly back up. Before she could get out a question, Korreth grasped her by the arms and with one swift pull, scooped her up. Zira released a surprised squeak as he set her in front of him on the saddle.

"What's your name, trainee?" Korreth demanded, his breath hot on her neck.

She shivered from the tickling sensation. "Zira."

"Well, *Zira*, looks like you're coming with me."

"Aren't we training here?" she asked, glancing at the other warriors and recruits who were entering the buildings.

"No." With that, Korreth brought the reins down and the creature took off on a heavy gallop. Zira's back struck the captain's broad chest as the beast's hooves pummeled the earth.

The freezing air hit her flesh and every hard inch of the captain was flushed with her. Each of his muscles flexed behind her as the reindeer picked up its pace, weaving around the icy forest. Alabaster trees filled with plump, deep blue fruit surrounded her. As the beast drove forward even faster, the white world became a blur, all except for the feel of the captain's strong body pressed to hers. It had been over a year since Zira had taken a lover to her bed. Not since Vron was slaughtered. Before him, she had only tumbled one other, a female—Leeana—who she'd been better off friends with. The one friend who she would also avenge.

As the beast hurled itself through the forest, snowflakes drifted from the sky, the shifting clouds the purest of whites. Not once had Zira been on a creature like this before. A stag, sure, a great white wolf, certainly, but this reindeer was more agile, stronger, than anything she'd ever ridden. The wind whipped around her face and her heart pounded. She closed her eyes for a moment, absorbing how free she felt.

Zira leaned back into the captain's touch, and even though he was a stranger, her body, her nerve endings, were all lit up in the moment. Like she was soaring through the sky.

Korreth tugged on the reins, the beast slowing to a stop, and Zira peeled open her eyes. In front of them stood a stone structure, snow covering its roof, and icicles clinging to the overhang.

With another swift motion, Korreth was off the beast and Zira in his arms. He lowered her to her feet, her breasts slowly sliding down his chest before he stepped back. She already missed the feel of his warmth.

The reindeer stepped toward her, and her eyes widened at its sharp teeth. But it nuzzled her neck and released a sweet, almost purring, sound.

"Dral." Korreth shot the beast a dirty look. The reindeer lifted its head and peered up at the captain with innocent eyes. "Return here before the sun sets."

Dral released a low grunt and nodded before darting off through the icy forest.

"Why aren't we training with the others?" Zira finally

said, staring at the structure. From the outside, it appeared no larger than a room inside her old home.

"It's your lucky day, remember?" Korreth arched a chestnut-colored brow that matched the curls in his hair. "You're with me. I train here." He scanned her over once more with that eyebrow of his still lifted. "Let's hope you can be trained within a week."

Zira would make it a priority before the end of the week. She hadn't expected to go out on a mission so soon, but this was even better, made the adrenaline and magic pump through her veins.

Korreth opened the door to the structure and she followed him inside. A rich pinewood scent enveloped her as she looked around. The room appeared more spacious inside than she'd expected. Other than iced, pale blue chains hanging across the walls, it was empty. She pulled a leather band from her pocket and quickly tied her loose hair into a braid down her back.

"What is your magic?" he asked.

"I can shape things from snow and water. You?"

"My magic pertains to battle, shifting ice and water into weapons, but we won't be focusing on our abilities today."

As Korreth sauntered to the center of the room, each of his muscles flexed, his pants tight across his ass. When he turned to face her, Zira's gaze drifted up, her cheeks flushing. He then cocked his head and held up a hand. "Get past my arm and hit me."

Zira took a deep swallow and studied his muscular arm as she stepped closer to him. She thrust a fist forward and with one quick motion, her hand was pinned to her back after he'd somehow spun her to face the opposite wall.

"Doesn't appear I was given a warrior," he said, and she could hear the annoyance in his voice.

Zira's nostrils flared. She yanked out of his grip, whirled around, and slammed a fist into his face. If she were outside, she would have created a snowball with her magic and slung it there next.

"Fuck!" Korreth shouted. He didn't even lift a hand to cover his eye where she'd struck.

"I know how to fight dirty." She shrugged. In her village, it was something that had to be done when her younger sisters had been picked on.

Zira waited to be reprimanded, to be sent back to the barracks, but instead, a deep chuckle escaped his pretty mouth. "So, you do have claws. Perhaps I can make a warrior out of you yet." He straightened once more, his face serious like before. "However, you need to know the basics. Changelings are smarter than you think and as I'm certain you're aware, immune to our influence." He lifted her arm, his calloused fingers brushing over her hand, sending tingles down her spine. "Now, let's begin with some blocks. When I bring my arm forward, pull yours up and stop mine. Like this." He moved his hand forward and tugged her arm to the side, letting them touch. "Understand?"

Zira nodded. It was simple enough.

As he threw his arm up, not going easy on her, she matched what he'd shown her, blocking his. She smirked.

"Hmm," Korreth said, his expression neutral.

Hmm? That was *it*? A little praise would be nice.

With a twist of the hips, and a shuffle of his feet, he now had Zira leaning forward, her head trapped in his grip. Her heart kicked at her sternum as she tried to shove him off.

"Find your way out of this, wild cat," Korreth drawled.

Zira would show him a wild cat... She contemplated slamming her fist into his cock this time, but she knew that wouldn't bode well, so she focused on another option. She pretended as though it was a changeling with its gangly arms around her. Their bodies appeared frail, yet their bones were as strong as iron, so fucking strong.

But as she yanked at Korreth's grip, she couldn't think of a way out. "I can't." She sighed, defeated.

"You can," he answered, confident. "Bend your knees, step with your right foot, turn toward it, keep your hands on my arm and twist out. Or you can put your hand on my face and sweep my legs out from under me."

The second option Zira liked more... She wanted to see the captain on his back. Perhaps in more ways than one... Naked... Sweaty... Her riding him... She shook off the enticing thought and focused. Pretended he was one of those changeling bastards. Bringing a hand to his face, she shoved at it as she swept his legs forward. Zira slipped out from Korreth's loosened hold while he fell backward and landed on his back with a hard blow.

"Good." He smiled, pushing himself to his feet. "Now, back up and lunge at me. We'll do a few of these exercises."

Something about this challenge shot a thrill through Zira. She took a step back and prepared herself as she looked at his handsome face, the sharp angles of his features, then at his broad chest, deciding where to strike.

Korreth lifted his brow and cocked his head. "We don't have all the time in the world, wild cat."

Clenching her teeth, Zira barreled toward him. He easily grabbed her by the waist, flipped her over, and tossed her to the floor. A sharp throb ran up her spine and she clenched her teeth harder to hold back her curses. Korreth hovered above, peering down at her. She wouldn't mind if he showed a bit of dominance—him on top, sliding into her with one easy thrust.

"Again," he demanded, voice deep, knocking her out of her pitiful thoughts.

And she did it again and again as he continued to throw her to the floor.

Time to fight dirty. She wished she'd hit him in his groin earlier when she'd had the chance. With narrowed eyes, she shot forward, but this time as his hands moved to her waist, she leaped through the air, knocking him back. Except, he took her down with him, gripping her by the waist. They fell to the floor together in one heavy heap. Her chest heaved against his, her lips dangerously close to brushing his. But she continued to pretend he was a changeling and pushed up so her legs straddled his narrow hips. With an imaginary blade in her hands, she lifted it and pressed the weapon into his chest, right at the heart. "Dead." She grinned.

Korreth licked his lips and smirked, one hand coming to her hip, the other at her throat. "Not dead, wild cat." He then slid a pretend blade across her flesh, his cock deliciously hardening beneath her. "Our next training step for tomorrow is how to kill a changeling."

3

KORRETH

Damn. Double damn. Triple, fucking, damn. As much as Korreth didn't want to think about his new trainee's body on top of his, there he was, standing next to his familiar, Dral, glowering at the tundra as if it were to blame.

After they were finished with their first lesson, he and Zira had left the training facility and, per his orders, she returned to the housing at the main barracks. Korreth refused to follow her. It was a difficult enough ride back as she rocked into him, only adding to his mounting desire. His blood coursed through him, hot, pounding, and he needed space to rein his control in.

Korreth had smelled the arousal on Zira and knew she'd felt his cock harden. It'd been far too long since he'd given in to his primal instinct, but this was different—the tug of a bond longing to be snapped into place was a maddening sensation, especially since they'd been so close to one another. He'd never felt it before, even with Orna, his childhood friend whom he'd tumbled. Korreth had cared for her, but there hadn't been a pulse in the air, or the yearning to pin her down and claim her as his own.

To say Zira was a minor inconvenience was an understatement. The changelings grew bolder and krampi were dying every day. Not to mention Major Enox had stormed onto the scene and taken control of his subordinates too. The last thing Korreth needed was Zira clouding his judgment.

Every time Korreth closed his eyes, he saw Zira's grinning face peering down at him. He heard the teasing sound of her panting breaths, daring him to push back, to explore what her limits were.

Growling, he shoved his fingers through his hair, avoiding his horns. "Fuck. I don't have time for this." He shifted, lowering a hand to reposition himself. Dral tilted his head, eyeing him with a widened red gaze. "Don't give me that. We don't all have the time to frolic around as you do." The reindeer sneezed in reply.

Korreth knew he couldn't remain outside forever. The snow fell steadily, leaving a blanket of white on top of his head. Korreth welcomed the cold. It chased away the heat searing through him. Eventually, he turned away from the tundra and led Dral toward the stable, where he untacked and fed the reindeer oats before he walked into the barracks.

The main meeting room was as sterile as the rest of the building. The gray walls would've been bare had it not been for the black, gnarled antlers that served as coat racks. Two long couches created an L shape in the middle of the room. Dark brown shelves lined the far wall, holding boots and a change of clothing for each warrior.

As luck would have it, Zira was nowhere to be seen, meaning he could slip into his quarters.

At the back of the room was a hallway, winding to a dark stairwell. It led to Korreth's apartment, which was larger than the simple housing of the other warriors. Korreth unbuttoned his leather uniform on the way upstairs. Phantom touches came unbidden, the featherlight caresses he wished were Zira's fingers skating over his abs, hips, and lower.

He shifted his gaze from the white ceiling to the black fur rug on the dark wooden floor. Instead of bare walls, skulls in various sizes decorated them, while others sat on black shelving, their empty eye sockets staring into the distance.

Shutting his door, he squeezed his eyes shut. His cock twitched to life once more, throbbing against the restraint of his leather pants. Korreth ground his teeth together as he sauntered into his living space and straight into the bathroom.

Even as the captain of the army, his bathroom was on the more simplistic side. The gray walls did nothing to brighten Korreth's mood, but the large porcelain tub sitting against the far wall beckoned him to it. He turned the water on and was greeted by steam as it touched the cool structure.

Stripping free of his uniform, he hung it on a pair of black antlers that stuck out from the wall. A flash of scarred skin on his chest caught his attention in the mirror. He'd earned each raised scar in battle or training, which was how he'd risen in the ranks to become captain. By the time Korreth reached the tub, it was full and ready for him. He stepped in, hissing as he lowered his body.

Korreth slipped beneath the water, allowing it to cover his head. The heat chased away the sultry image of Zira's hips rocking against him, but it was only a temporary fix as his body grew accustomed to the temperature.

When he surfaced, he slapped the side of the tub, the

sound reverberating off the walls. "Dammit!" he growled, snatching up a washcloth from the shelf next to the tub, and did something he seldom allowed himself to do—give in. Korreth pushed his hand into the water and circled his fingers around his length, pumping himself steadily.

With his eyes wrenched shut, Korreth's head lolled back. He imagined Zira on her knees, in front of him with a wild grin on her face as she took his tip into her mouth. He groaned, feeling a tightening begin in his abdomen, in his balls.

But Korreth didn't want Zira to only suck him off. He wanted to plunge into her depths. He wanted to smell the heady, minty scent of their sexes joining and lap up her arousal as she screamed his name over and over.

He tightened his grip and quickened his motions, rubbing his thumb along the throbbing tip. Korreth's eyebrows drew inward the moment pleasure unfolded in him. He hissed as he came to the luscious images of Zira playing through his mind.

Korreth's body quaked with pleasure, and he drank in deep breaths, his chest heaving. Did Zira feel the tug of the bond, too? Or was it simply him? Perhaps he had been affected so much because he didn't make it a practice to fuck every female who walked his way. There were consequences to that if one wasn't careful.

A pounding on his door sounded, pulling him to attention. Not sparing a minute, he leaped from the tub and grabbed two towels. One, he wrapped around his lean waist, and the other, he ran through his hair while striding into the main room. When he got to the door, the one he'd used on his hair fell around his shoulders. He yanked open the door, only to find the face that had driven him to climaxing moments ago.

Zira's tight expression coupled with the way she rasped, "Captain," set every one of his nerves on edge. "It's the changelings, they slaughtered—"

Without waiting to hear the rest of what Zira was about to say, Korreth ran into his room and grabbed a fresh uniform. Not unlike so many krampi, Korreth had a grudge against changelings, too. They'd slain someone close to him.

As long as the changelings fought against them, they served no purpose other than destruction. Never once had they sought peace. They were creatures of deception and ruin.

Korreth wanted to eradicate them.

Storming out of his room, he stared at Zira, who'd let herself into his quarters. Indignation burned him. *How dare she invite herself into his space?* "I don't remember inviting you in, wild cat," he ground out as he quickly buttoned the front of his uniform.

Zira scoffed. "Nor did you ask for the rest of my statement." She cocked her hip before heading toward the door. "Warriors have returned, if you want to call it returning. They're shredded." Her voice broke as she said the last word, but she seemed to swallow whatever emotion had crept up.

Korreth admired that. If he had to guess, she'd lost someone dear to her because of the blasted changelings. The numbers of those affected by them seemed to grow every day.

Motioning to the door, he tilted his head and lifted a brow. "If you put a little more effort into your footsteps and less in that loose tongue of yours, you'd almost be out the door by now." Except, he wanted to desperately put that tongue to use. In his mouth, on his cock, anywhere on his body.

Zira slanted him a look. Her dark brown eyes cutting through him at the same time the scent of her did. She still hadn't washed up. Her sweat and the delicate fragrance of mint wafted from her.

Korreth, in return, shot her a bland expression and reached over her head to grab a coiled leather whip from a shelf next to the door. He leaned in, too close to her. "Move. Your. Ass." Zira jerked away and ran down the stairwell. Korreth took a moment to fully appreciate her curves before he jogged after her.

"Where were they—" The question died on his tongue as he followed her out of the building and into the training yard. Krampi bodies were strewn on makeshift cots, laid down carefully on the freshly fallen snow.

Korreth recognized a female in particular—Nisa. One arm was missing, her face gashed open. Her stomach revealed a hole, and beside her, rested a pile of her entrails. Blood as dark as the night sky painted the ground, permeating the air with a metallic tinge. Nisa had been a fierce warrior, and one of Korreth's proteges. Although hardened by his years in the ranks, the sight was enough to spark his ire.

Every muscle in his body tightened. Another friend slaughtered. Another krampi dead. Enough was enough.

He turned to Zira, whose face had turned ashen. A word of comfort lingered on the tip of his tongue, but she wasn't looking at him.

The other recruits gathered around, murmuring their respects to the fallen warriors.

A low growl escaped him as he gripped onto the leather whip tighter. "Finish tending to them and notify their families at once. Go with peace and honor, my brothers and sisters, you fought well." Korreth bowed to the fallen krampi, then turned on his heel, not checking to see if Zira or the other recruits even followed him.

The distinct sound of several feet shuffling behind him told him she did, in fact, pursue him, as did the others. But if Zira knew what was good for her, she wouldn't want to. "I'll warn you once to return to the barracks. That is your one warning before you see how we handle these wretched fucks." He twisted at the waist to watch her contemplate it for a moment, then her jaw hardened.

Zira's gaze locked on his. "No. I want to see them suffer." Behind her, a few recruits turned around, but most stuck by.

Korreth nodded and continued walking toward the giant furnace located across the training yard. Behind the barrack building, a spiral column jutted toward the sky, and sparks spat upward. At first glance, the furnace could be mistaken for a watchtower, but with smoke billowing from it, and not a speck of snow in the immediate area, it was clear the structure emitted heat. In the belly of it was a pit of fire that never extinguished, nor was it ever sated.

Even from several hundred yards away, the lick of heat skimmed his cheek and burned his eyes.

"It's so hot," Zira murmured.

"Not hot enough." Korreth seethed as he strode forward. Two krampi warriors held a writhing changeling while it screamed. It sounded much like a fork scraping against a plate. Ear-splitting and sickening. The creature's pale, waxy arms flailed, its elongated fingers clawing in desperation at the warriors holding it. Aside from the wide, yellow eyes without pupils, there were no specific features of its face. Every changeling held a mouth that looked sewn together by its own flesh. The only difference was the shade of wispy hair on their head.

Casting its eyes on Korreth, it let out another nasty scream. A black tongue swirled behind the slits where lips should've been. No doubt it longed to claim and change into something other than itself. Changelings could thrive in their true form, but their restlessness drove them to find bodies to possess, and krampi weren't compatible with them. However, they were fond of what they possessed. Land, weapons, and power.

The changelings opted to infiltrate the human world and focused on weak prey: mortal children. Korreth detested the creatures before but knowing they purposely targeted children was unforgivable.

"Captain Korreth!" a warrior bellowed. Rizaron—Nisa's mate—approached with a reddened face. "There are more changelings being carted up, but this one attacked Nisa's party. I saw it—" Rizaron choked on the words. "Do your worst, Captain." He bowed his head and motioned with his hand toward the whipping pole. The structure was crafted of white pine, but dried blood had long since stained the once pristine wood, painting it bluish-black. It stretched to a full six feet in height, then a shorter pole ran across the top where the changeling's arms strapped into place. On the bottom, there were also straps to secure the legs.

"Do you know what the pole is for?" he asked Zira, who'd sidled up to his side.

A look of uncertainty passed over her face as she frowned. "I thought it was pretty clear it's for punishment."

Korreth nodded. "Partly." He unfurled the whip while he approached the post. The changeling writhed and screamed against the pole. "When a changeling takes on the body of another species, it must be separated. Extreme pain divides them from the life they assumed, because to outright kill one would destroy two lives. We only want these useless blackguards to suffer. So, we whip them until they relinquish their hold on the other life before we burn them, to ensure they cannot procreate or do it again."

"But this one hasn't…" Zira silenced herself and Korreth assumed it was because she caught the meaning. This changeling was meant to suffer, whether or not it stole a body, it still stole a life.

Korreth glanced her way one last time, to the rest of the recruits, then jerked his head. "Move aside, Zira." His voice came out in a growl, and she acquiesced. Lifting his arm, he slashed through the air with the whip, and it smacked the changeling's papery thin skin. A high-pitched screech emitted, piercing Korreth's ears. In the wake of the lash, a streak of blue blood trickled down the changeling's spine and dripped to the gray, stone ground.

Again and again, Korreth struck the creature. A few recruits retched behind him, but he didn't take note of who it was, or whose hurried footsteps carried away. He lost himself to the lashings until the changeling sagged to the ground, its back torn to shreds, just as it had torn Nisa apart.

"Drag its corpse to the furnace," Korreth ordered in between panting. His chest heaved with the exertion while sweat trickled down his brow and licked at his temples. He sauntered away and found a puddle to clean off the bits of sinew and blood coating the whip.

"With pleasure," Rizaron replied, his eyes lingering on Korreth's, silently thanking him for the pound of flesh he'd taken. It wouldn't bring Nisa back, but justice had been served. Then, Rizaron and his comrade unwound the changeling's bindings and carried it toward the entry hall that led to the stairs of the drop-off point of the furnace.

Once Korreth cleaned his whip and wound it around his hand again, he turned to look at the remaining recruits and zeroed in on Zira. "Any questions?"

4

ZIRA

Korreth asked the group of recruits if they had any questions. Zira had plenty of questions for the captain. Mostly, she wanted to know when she could borrow his whip and slam it down on a changeling herself. With each lash against the changeling's flesh, Zira had felt a heat spread straight to her core. The way the captain had brought that bastard down, it had been almost as good as when she'd felt his cock pressed to her while training. Neither had mentioned anything about that enticing incident. Not after they'd been interrupted by the sound of Dral's hoofbeats when the reindeer had come back to meet them.

As she peered out at what was left of the shriveled changeling in one of the warrior's arms, its navy blood splattered across the snow, Zira raised her hand.

Korreth scanned the other recruits as though searching to answer someone else's question, but no one lifted their hand. He sighed, his pale blue eyes meeting hers. "Yes, Zira?"

Straightening her shoulders, she took a step toward him.

"Are you not going to kill it?" Eventually, the thing would wake and heal—they always did.

The captain arched a brow, the edges of his lips tilting up to one side. "Today, all of you recruits get to witness the changeling's demise in the furnace."

A gleefulness spread through her. She knew changelings died from fire, but she had never seen one trapped in flames before. Grinning, she peered around the group and her smile slipped. Most of the surrounding recruits' eyes filled with horror. Several of them had already spilled their earlier meals in the snow while watching the changeling's whipping. But if the recruits couldn't handle any of this, then how were they supposed to kill the creatures on their own?

"Any other questions before we start?" Korreth asked, his voice assertive.

The recruits shook their heads. Zira had several but seeing how a changeling was truly defeated was more important for now.

Korreth motioned them to follow him toward the furnace. The slush beneath Zira's boots became water as she drew closer and peered up at the structure. It wasn't a small furnace either. Ivory iron covered the outside walls, and a triangular roof with a curving chimney rested on top. Thick smoke billowed out from the chimney, and the heat radiated from its depths, brushing her skin.

"Who would like to do the honor of opening and closing the door?" Korreth may have spoken to all the recruits, but his eyes were fixed on hers, daring.

Zira raised her hand again, and he gestured her forward with a finger. A finger that she wanted to taste and run her tongue up. She pushed the thought away, focusing on the rush flowing through her veins, because she would be the one to usher in the changeling's demise.

The warrior holding the limp creature shifted beside her, and Zira inhaled, catching the stench of the changeling's body. Decay and uncleanliness—pure filth.

Korreth gave Zira an encouraging nod as they walked up the stairs together. She grabbed the warm metal handle, then pulled open the large door with a resounding creak. Bright blue flames crawled up the walls, stretching from the endless pit below, crackling as if speaking their own language. If necessary, countless changelings could be tossed inside the furnace at one time. All krampi could use the power of influence, but it was too bad it didn't work on changelings, or she would have instructed them to walk off the ledge and burn. That particular ability only worked on certain species, though.

The warrior tossed the changeling into the fire with a *thump*. Zira slammed the door shut, bolting the latch.

Taking a step back, she studied the furnace and wished it were made of glass so she could see inside, confirming that the flames were indeed doing their duty.

A horrible screech wailed from the depths—the creature had roused from its sleep. An ear-piercing, grating noise bounced off the iron walls, a sound Zira knew to be nails swiping in desperation.

"Will it climb to the top?" Zira glanced at the captain, her eyes growing wide.

"Not before it dies," Korreth said, his voice assured.

The changeling fought for its life for a little while longer before its screams slowly died, the flames inside melting and licking away its flesh. An odor permeated the air, and she covered her nose—rot combined with melted flesh. The recruits didn't make a single sound, only watched. A few trembled, their mouths agape. However, the warriors remained in a straight position, their expressions neutral, seeming to be used to this. Zira relished this moment, wishing there was another to toss in.

After a few more silent seconds, Korreth cleared his throat and faced the recruits. "This concludes your training for the day. When the sun rises in the morning, you will meet here for more training. Our time is limited, so the hours will be long." He turned to Zira and leaned forward, her heart pounding at his nearness, his pinewood scent. "As for you, wild cat," he whispered in a gruff voice, "have a good evening."

With that, Korreth sauntered away. Zira furrowed her brow while studying his tight ass, thinking about their earlier ride back on Dral after their training session, when the captain had acted stiff once more. But here he was now calling her wild cat again.

Zira thought about the changeling as she walked inside the barracks and headed to the washroom. She wondered if the changelings even had families in their nests—they always seemed so hostile, even to one another.

Bunk beds filled the large space of the barracks with not much else besides the pale white walls and the skulls of changelings hanging as decoration. Zira had only been inside here for a little while since she'd returned from training with Korreth. It had given her enough time to claim a bed and grab a trunk of clothing, which each recruit was given. She hadn't brought any clothing from home. There was nothing she'd wanted to take anyway besides a small music box that had belonged to her sisters, Sersha and Pila. The warriors had told her she would be provided everything she needed.

Most of the recruits were changing into their night clothing as Zira knelt in front of her trunk.

"You can have the bottom bed if you want," a female said, her voice soft.

She glanced at the other female kneeling beside her, one of her horns broken. "It's okay." Zira smiled. "I don't mind taking the top."

"I'm Luna." The female was small with bright green eyes and dark hair—something about her reminded Zira of her youngest sister, Pila.

"Zira." She brought a fist to her chest. "I'm going to bathe." Blowing out a breath, she then walked away, not wanting to continue seeing her sister in this young krampi's face. She didn't want to think about her family right now— she had to focus.

The door to the washroom was already wide open. Inside, a light fog wafted through the air, rising from rows of iron bathtubs. Zira grabbed a soap bar and towel before peeling off her clothing. She stepped inside a bathtub near a far wall, absorbing the warmth of the water. Releasing a relaxed sound, she cleaned herself with a soap bar. Her muscles were tight and sore, the training from the day finally catching up to her.

She toyed with the water for a moment, letting her magic flow through her as she pulled a few droplets into the air, freezing them, then shaping them into a tiny snowflake. Sighing, she let the snowflake fall back into the water and break apart.

After she finished cleaning and getting dressed, Zira padded back into the sleeping area. Only a dim blue light from the ceiling guided her way to her bunk. She crawled in and peered up at the ceiling, watching the shadows from the flames dance.

"Did you see how the captain easily cracked the whip down on the changeling?" a female asked another krampi.

"He terrifies me," another female answered.

"I'd fuck him all night though."

Zira stilled and inwardly growled at the words. If anyone was going to ride the captain all night long, it would be her. And then as she closed her eyes to sleep, she imagined her naked body sinking down on him in the training room where she'd felt his hard cock against her.

Zira sat fully dressed on her bed, eating a pomegranate. It tasted fresh and the flavor was better than any fruit she'd had back at home, so she'd taken several from the barrel a warrior had brought in. After chewing the last few seeds, she followed the other recruits into the morning light.

The cool breeze ruffled the ends of her braid, and the burning scent of the changeling was long gone. Her gaze caught on a group of warriors standing with their arms behind their backs, their legs parted, and in the center was Korreth. The wind deliciously rumpled his hair and her heart leaped as she scanned his body, the way his uniform hugged each hard muscle. *Focus, Zira.*

"Before training begins," Korreth said, taking a step forward. "I will need to discuss the mortal world with you all. For those who do not know, when one enters it, humans will not see you as you are. They see more than our horns, they see vicious, fur-covered beasts with forked tongues and fangs that the humans believe to be a mythical creature known as Krampus. If you are spotted, you will need to use your influence on them. Control their minds and make them forget."

A human wouldn't see her as she was? Zira hadn't known this, and more questions filled her head. She raised her hand.

"Yes, Zira." Korreth sighed.

"Do the humans still see us as beasts if they were to come here?"

"No."

Strange.

"So today," Korreth continued, "we will test your stealth. You will go into the forest behind the barracks and hide. The last one who I find won't have to finish training outside. As I locate each of you, return here and begin push-ups until your training warrior approaches you."

"Hide in the forest?" a tall female said, her shirt tight across her breasts. "It's like a childhood game."

"These aren't games." Korreth narrowed his eyes. "Humans may have weaknesses, but their weapons do not. Now go and stay inside the rope barrier. You have three minutes." His gaze lingered on Zira for a second, her breath catching, before he turned to face the other direction.

Three minutes? Zira whirled around and sprinted through the snow toward the forest. The sun shone brightly as she halted at the edge of the forest in front of rows of sky-scraping ivory trees. The rope didn't leave them many options for hiding since the space was perhaps the size of a couple barracks put together. The last time she'd played a game of hide and seek was with her younger sisters when they were smaller. A dark thought entered her mind—she wondered where they and her parents had hidden before being slaughtered.

Shrugging off the image, she watched as the other recruits chose spaces behind trunks and boulders. The branches were too high for most to grab, but Zira was good at climbing. Taking a breath, she hurled herself toward an alabaster tree, pushed on it with her boot, and kicked her body upward. She easily grabbed a branch and pulled herself onto it. Just as she settled atop the limb, blending in with the pale leaves, Korreth appeared.

Somehow, he managed to keep every one of his movements light. There wasn't any sound from his boots against the snowy ground, even as he trekked over fallen leaves. He remained quiet while easily picking out one recruit after another, not saying a single word to any of them as they headed back to train.

And then, no one was in the forest except for the two of them. Zira grinned, keeping silent as he crept around the forest, his hands skimming across the trunks.

"Wild cat, get your ass down from the tree," Korreth finally said, peering up at her with a smirk. "I knew you were there from the moment I stepped into the forest."

"But there's a good reason for choosing the top of a tree." Her grin grew wider when he halted beneath her.

He arched a brow. "And why's that?"

"This!" Zira leaped from the branch, colliding with his body. He fell to his back, taking her with him. She snatched his arms and pressed them to his sides.

"Ah." He chuckled before flipping her over, holding her down. "That move may work on a human but not on me. I'm starting to believe you just want me on the ground."

What she wanted was to circle her legs around his hips and grind herself against his hard length. "If you knew where I was, then why didn't you say anything?"

"You don't feel it, do you?" he rasped, his eyes turning serious.

Feel what? All she felt was his hard body against hers. "I don't understand."

He sighed, peeling himself from Zira and holding his hand out for her. "Come on, we'll go inside for mental training today."

It had been a while since she truly spent time indoors. "All right." She gripped his hand and pushed herself up. "Are we going to see Dral today?"

"Miss him already?" Korreth smirked.

"Yes. *He's* at least nice." She grinned and winked at him.

"What? I'm nice."

"Perhaps." Zira stayed smiling as he led her out of the forest to a tall rectangular structure across from the barracks. She wondered if Korreth had ever been close to claiming a mate. His neck and shoulders were always hidden, but she believed he hadn't been. However, that didn't mean he didn't fuck when he felt like it.

Korreth held open the door as she walked inside to a large room, where several warriors sat in padded chairs, chatting softly and eating fruit. He opened another door and led her into an area with fur blankets sprawled across the floor. A bright blue fire burned inside a fireplace, giving off a comforting heat to her flesh. Her heart beat faster at the calming sight.

"This is the mental room," he said, shutting the door behind him. "It's to help you train and relax your mind."

Relax? If anything, she wanted to have her way with him right here on the fur rug.

Korreth took a seat in front of the fire and patted the spot beside him. "Tell me why you hate the changelings so much."

Blowing out a breath, she sank down next to him, her knees brushing his. "Besides the obvious, they murdered everyone I love."

His gaze locked on hers, and his expression softened. "I've lost people too, but you have to watch your drive. It can't be only about vengeance. That will make you weak. You need to want it not only for your desire, but for the safety of our world, the human world."

Zira rolled her eyes. "I do."

He cocked his head and blinked at her as though he could see deep down into her mind.

"All right," she muttered. "It's for vengeance, but not only that. When you mentioned yesterday the part about innocent children being taken, their lives stolen, I wouldn't want that for anyone's child. Besides that, even if they don't wear our children's skin, they kill them. If you had a child, could you imagine what that would be like for the demons to rip out their lungs and tear off their limbs?"

Korreth's brow furrowed. "I would peel off strips of their flesh, piece by piece, with my bare hands."

As Zira went to speak, the captain changed the subject, "We have training to do. Close your eyes."

For the next two days, Korreth stayed rigid, professional, training Zira hard. Both physically and mentally. She learned fast, and so did most of the recruits. A couple were sent home after not being able to improve quickly—they would have only made the task harder on the warriors. They weren't meant for this life. But Zira felt this was what she was born to be.

A warrior.

Korreth placed a heavy ice chain over her shoulder, his fingertips brushing her neck. Her eyes fluttered at the touch. He then rested the end of the chain in her hands.

"Bring the changeling to the center of the circle," he instructed, taking a step back.

Zira peered at the fake creature weaved together from tree branches. "Can we use a real one instead?"

"Eventually, wild cat. Mirror what I do." He lifted his own ice chain and swung it in the air, the muscles of his arms flexing, his hips making small sensual circles. Heat coursed through her as she watched him, her body igniting with the fire of desire.

Then he launched the chain forward, the clanking echoing as it circled the branched object. He easily yanked it to the center of the circle.

Damn. He truly was a son of Morozko.

Taking a deep swallow, collecting herself, Zira gripped her chain and swung it around and around, the way Korreth had shown her a moment ago. Particles of snow lifted from the ground as her magic came alive. Ignoring it, she cracked the chain forward like a whip, a loud voice boomed from behind her and she stumbled.

"Warriors and recruits," Major Enox shouted, stepping out from a barrack, his dark hair neatly behind his shoulders. "Change of plans. The enemy nest has hatched, and the changelings have already intercepted around twenty mortal children's bodies. Each of you will be given a location to retrieve a child and bring them back. Then you will beat the asshole changeling until it splits away from those innocent mortal children."

Zira was ready—ready to fight. Korreth slanted a look her way and gave her a brief nod, as though he believed she was ready too.

5

KORRETH

KORRETH SHIFTED HIS JAW, WAITING FOR ENOX TO ASSIGN THE krampi that would make the journey to the mortal realm with him. His eyes found Zira's and within the dark depths of her gaze, he saw a question. *So soon?* But Zira and the rest of the recruits were ready enough for the mission. They'd have to be.

Korreth would be lying if he said Zira hadn't impressed him over the past few days of training. She took to it with ease and twisted it into a game while they grappled. What rankled him was how she felt beneath him, how she stirred a primal instinct in him. Not just desire, but a *need* to claim her, to sink into her depths and fill her to the brim with his throbbing cock.

He'd felt the tug of lust before and had rutted like a young buck in his earlier years, but he'd never felt the need to claim before. The thunderous pulse of it in his veins and in his chest was new to him.

Finally, Enox addressed him. "Captain, since the recruits have done so well with their training, I believe it's wise to send them off with their mentor. Which means you'll be taking your trainee to the mortal realm."

An argument formed on the tip of Korreth's tongue. Zira would serve as a distraction, and it wasn't simply the curve of her hip or the swell of her breasts that enticed him. Zira's scent and the feel of her body aligning with his—it was driving him mad.

It was also why the bond usually worked *both ways*. At least, that was what he'd been told by others. Did she truly not feel the tug, or was she taunting him?

"Yes, Major," he grunted. "When are we moving out?"

"Immediately. Pack the supplies needed in the sleighs, but you'll all be leaving within the day." Enox turned on his heel, his long, dark tresses rustling in the frigid wind. "Get a move on. Now."

"Wait, Major," Korreth blurted before he could walk away. "Relay to Aeryx that I love him, and that I'll return as swiftly as possible." His gaze lingered on the major. The last thing he wanted to do was talk about Aeryx to Zira, and he assumed her curious mind would want answers.

Enox nodded. "You have my word." He sauntered away without so much as looking over his shoulder.

Zira shifted at Korreth's side and when their eyes met again, she nodded. "Tell me what I need to do, and I can help."

"Oh, you don't have a choice in the matter," Korreth rumbled as he glanced past her and toward the stables. He ignored the indignant huff from Zira and continued, "Before we head to the stables, we need provisions. Food, bedrolls, and water. It could take a few days for us to complete this mission, and we should prepare for that." It wasn't always the changelings that made things difficult. The mortals were a restless species, and they were also keen on protecting themselves. They possessed house alarms, attack dogs, and guns. He'd experienced all the above, including a dog chomping down on his leg.

"Does it usually take so long?"

Korreth shook his head. "No, it usually only takes a night, but sometimes the mortals get in the way, and it'll take longer."

Krampi didn't need firearms. They had brute strength and speed, not to mention, magic. Even a simple burst of icy air tumbling toward a mortal was enough to knock them down.

"Let's go." He jerked his head toward the barrack building, where their supplies were housed. Snow crunched beneath his footfall and though he wished to remain quiet as he worked, Zira spoke up.

"What will we do when we cross into the mortal land? How do we know where to go?" She jogged up to him, stepping just enough in front of him so that she was in his line of vision. Red painted her cheeks and excitement glittered in her eyes.

"The stone will let us know because it'll home in on their magic. Each stone is imbued with the essence of a changeling, and it helps us locate them, even in the mortal realm. Consider them a fox, and we are the hounds chasing them down."

Zira's eyebrows furrowed. "They're not foxes. Foxes serve a purpose—they keep pests under control and balance life, while changelings don't. The changelings are creatures of chaos and destruction."

"Be careful with your anger, it can blind you," he reminded her. "I'm sure once they served as much purpose as a fox, but time and difficulties have a way of twisting things beyond recognition." Korreth tilted his head as Zira paused in her jogging, her face twisting into an expression of frustration. "Don't confuse my words for sticking up for them. You know I lose no sleep over those bastards."

"I wouldn't know, Captain. I've never been in your bed, but if you'd prefer that to change…" Zira purred her words, and it was like oil to the flame of his desire.

Korreth stopped in his tracks, and, in a flash of movement, his forefinger and thumb caught her chin. He leaned in close enough so that he could nearly taste her inviting lips. "And what would you do in my bed, wild cat?" His eyes searched hers, which were currently wide, but her hands instinctively reached out to press against his chest. "Tell me, I'm all ears."

As Korreth watched her, crimson rushed into her cheeks, and it wasn't from running. Whether or not she'd ever tumbled with a male, he didn't know, but what Korreth did know was that Zira didn't shy away from a situation.

Unspoken words flickered in her gaze and the playful tilt of her lips told him it had nothing to do with the mission at hand. Disappointingly, she kept them to herself.

He shifted his jaw and reluctantly released her chin as he glanced down at her bare neck. No mark claiming her, and her flesh seemed intent on reminding him of the call of their bond.

Zira's hands slipped down his chest before falling to her sides. "We don't have enough time for me to wax poetic about what I'd do."

Korreth took a step backward and shook his head as he stormed off toward the supply building. In truth, he didn't want to hear the words tumble from those pretty lips. He wanted to put that mouth to use by filling it with his hard cock until her tongue sent him over the edge and he came undone.

Shit. Stop thinking about it, you fool. He shook his head again, clearing his thoughts as he sauntered inside the building. Not unlike the living quarters, it was sterile and pristine. Instead of gray walls, they were white, with ivory pine shelving that ran the length of the room. "Grab the bag on the wall." He pointed to where several empty ones hung. Korreth opted for two pairs of iron cuffs, a whip, and two daggers. He tossed them into the bag as Zira presented it to him.

After, he took her to the back room where the food storage was. Instead of walls of shelving, this one was full of white pine tables, with woven baskets of jerky and canteens of water resting atop. When they had enough, he led Zira out the back door toward the stable.

"Captain," Zira broke through the silence. "What is it like in the mortal world?"

"You'll see soon enough, but their winters, mostly, are nothing like Frosteria. Sometimes, there isn't even snow." He chuckled at her look of disbelief. "Imagine a land where it's as hot as the furnace. I've been there."

They entered the stable, and the scent of pine shavings filled the air, mixing with the musk of the reindeer. Warriors milled around, fetching their mounts and sleighs.

Korreth sauntered toward Dral's stall, then glanced back at Zira. "I trust you know how to tack up a reindeer?" he asked dryly as he spun to face her.

Zira rolled her eyes. "Of course I do."

Korreth took the supply bag from her and arched a brow.

"Just because I'm not a warrior doesn't mean I'm inept,

Captain." She reached toward the bridle hanging from black stag antlers on the stall door.

Her response prompted a crooked smile from him before he turned toward the open aisle. "Tack up Dral, and I'll fetch the sleigh. Meet me out front."

Korreth approached the sleigh. It was simple in comparison to the more elaborately designed ones. The runners consisted of black iron that curled in the front and melded into the frame of the structure. Even the bench seat was black leather. The only hint of color on the sleigh was the cargo area in the back, which was coated by a piece of red fabric.

Without so much of a glance downward, Korreth threw their packs in the sleigh with their supplies and weapons, in case things didn't go according to plan. Although he didn't expect things to go awry, there was always the distinct possibility it could happen.

He glanced up at the sound of approaching footsteps. Zira led Dral toward him and motioned to his familiar, who let out a whuffle of breath that sounded too much like a laugh. One quick glance at the reindeer's equipment and he saw she did, in fact, properly tack him up.

"Well, wild cat, looks like you managed it." He reached out to snag Dral's harness and chuckled. "Hop into the sleigh. We don't have time to waste." Korreth finished strapping Dral to the front of the sleigh, then joined Zira on the leather seat. His shoulder brushed against hers and he willed his mounting arousal from earlier back down.

"And off we go, Captain?" Zira met his gaze and smirked.

Korreth turned away, glancing skyward at the night's stars shining above him. *Morozko give him the strength to ignore the female.* If luck were on his side, the journey would be a quick one, but considering who his current companion was, chances were it'd be the longest trip he'd ever been on.

"Dash away, dash away," he murmured dryly to Zira, then shifted his attention to the horizon. Dral's hooves churned up the snow and ice as he pulled them down the sloping terrain of the fortress.

It was a little ways before they arrived where Korreth typically summoned the portal. He lifted his hand and drew a circle in the air, concentrating on opening it. The magic pulled at him, drinking away a fraction of his power, and in a blink, before them, a swirling image of another world shimmered. It was night there, just as it was in Frosteria. Blue flames licked around the edges, writhing like a living creature. Within the center, a silver color with white specks glowed.

Clucking his tongue, Korreth shifted the reins forward. "Walk on," he ordered Dral.

And through the portal they went.

Some krampi would end up in the same part of the mortal realm, while others would wind up in an entirely different part of the world.

Korreth was used to it, the uneasy feeling in his belly and the disorienting tug as the energy of their world faded away and turned into the dullness of the mortal realm.

Dral's hooves crunched ice as he pulled the sleigh toward the line of trees before them. Snow blanketed evergreens and the ground. To the eye, it didn't differ from the landscape of home, but the sounds of vehicles driving by, and the distant wailing of a train's horn, proved otherwise.

Even though trees surrounded them, mortal life thrived behind the tree line. An entire town bustled on the other side. Korreth turned to glance over the rail of the sleigh and spotted train tracks. He urged Dral to shift forward until they were nearly inside the forest.

"What's that noise?" Zira hissed. She stirred by his side, twisting to peer around.

He grinned. "The sound of humans." Korreth's eyes narrowed on her face as he took in her expression. She didn't look ill, but he wanted to make sure. "How is your stomach?"

"It's fine—or will be—that wailing is normal here?"

"Ah, yes. It beats the alternative, which is no warning of what is to follow." Korreth dipped his hand into his jacket's pocket and drew out a stone. While he could use his magic in the realm of mortals, it was easier when it was focused on a stone. His gaze flicked toward Zira, who'd spun around on the seat to see where the wailing had originated from.

Her nose scrunched up in confusion. "What?"

"Well—" The ground shook violently, interrupting Korreth. A thunderous whoosh of air followed as a train flew by, blaring its horn loud enough that it silenced Zira's shriek.

"You could have warned me!" She smacked his chest with an open hand, which pulled a chuckle from him. As she yanked her hand away, he snatched her wrist and tugged her closer to him.

"But there was simply no time at all for that." He grinned, even as heat flooded his belly and coursed through his veins. Zira had teased him a fair amount during their time together and if he'd read the situations properly, she wouldn't have been opposed to a quick fuck.

The moon wasn't nearly high enough, and the realm was still far too active for them to venture into the town yet. They had time to spare.

Korreth released Zira's hand, then glanced down at the

stone, pulsing a soft white. The stone was drawn to the specific magical components of a changeling and as they drew closer, the light would blink faster.

"Now we make camp. Typically, we wait until after midnight to advance on the changeling." He took one look up at the moon and surmised it was around nine o'clock at night.

"Here?" She glanced around, her brow furrowing. "In the open?"

It was quiet and Korreth couldn't hear anyone approaching. A rare emotion ignited within him: mischief. Surely Zira would appreciate the sentiment... and if not... He cleared his throat.

"Yes, right here." He leaned back, watching Zira hop down from the sleigh. Korreth almost felt a twinge of guilt tug at him while Zira's face scrunched up in bewilderment. She wanted so badly to succeed at this mission, he could tell, and for that, Korreth respected her.

She turned her head side to side, squinting at the landscape. "It seems rather... vulnerable out in the open."

"You're right, wild cat, we should go deeper in the forest." Korreth clucked to Dral, who pulled the sleigh ahead at a slow pace. Zira yelped in complaint as she jogged alongside them. It wasn't a fast pace. She could've grabbed the sleigh's railing and pulled herself in, but she ran beside him, scowling.

"Wait!" she huffed in annoyance, which only amused Korreth.

Once they were deep enough in the forest, Korreth halted Dral, then hopped down from the sleigh. Much to his surprise, Zira didn't stop jogging until she was right in front of him, her chest heaving and her cheeks red from the effort of running.

His gaze dropped to the swell of her breasts, which was unfortunately hidden but not indistinguishable.

This time, when she lifted her hand to him, he was ready and as she went to strike him, he flipped her arm behind her back and pinned it there. Zira was quick though and slid one of her legs between his to knock Korreth off balance. He pitched forward, which was enough for her to kick his leg to the side.

Zira yanked out of his grasp, but before she could launch another attack at him, he shoved her to the ground, using his weight to his advantage. Korreth restrained her legs with his, then he grabbed her flailing arms and bound them above her head.

She glared up at him and as he was readying to speak, he scarcely missed the cue of her head lifting. Zira rammed into his shoulder, producing a groan from him. Korreth transferred his grip on her wrists into one hand.

"Need I fucking remind you of your place, wild cat?" he growled.

Zira's hips bucked beneath him, attempting to shift his weight off her, but he didn't budge.

"And where is that exactly, Captain?" Although she was glaring at him, he could sense the shift in her demeanor and the heat filling her eyes.

As Zira's tongue darted out to wet her lips, Korreth lowered his head, her hot breath mingling with his. His pants grew tighter with each movement of her breasts against his chest and the primal piece of him wanted to shred the leather binding her, hiding the tender pieces of her body from him. And when he could no longer restrain himself, Korreth gave in to Zira's tempting lips and crashed his mouth to hers.

She stilled at first, and he wondered if he'd made a mistake, but then her lips parted, and the tension released from her form as Zira's tongue brushed against his.

He groaned, the taste of her filling his senses. Korreth's grip loosened on her wrists and immediately her hands threaded through his hair. Beneath him, she shifted, and his length pressed into her. She sucked in a breath, moaning into his mouth, and he rolled his hips forward.

"What are you waiting for?" Zira taunted, biting his bottom lip.

Fuck. Korreth pulled back and glanced down at her. His better senses told him to refrain, but with the call of the bond and the feel of her warmth radiating onto his throbbing member, he wasn't about to abstain.

"I was waiting for you to wax poetic about *how* you wanted it." But before Zira could reply with a barb, Korreth claimed her lips again and moved into a kneeling position so he could begin undoing her leather breeches.

His fingers skimmed the soft flesh of her abdomen, then as his knuckles dragged downward, inside her pants, brushing against her mound, it was Zira who cursed. She trembled in want as his fingers dipped lower, slipping along her heated seam to rub teasingly. He wanted to taste her with his tongue—he wanted his cock inside her, feeling every inch of her while he thrust, while he ignited their mating bond.

"Enough with the teasing, Captain." Zira's words came out breathlessly as her hands slid up to his vest to undo it.

"There will be no teasing, but we have a few hours to kill, and I am nothing if not a thorough male." His voice rumbled as he rubbed the sensitive ball of nerves. Zira's eyes slammed shut and she released a deep moan.

She raked her nails down the hollow of his throat, eliciting a growl from him.

Korreth removed his hand from her heat, readying to yank down her breeches, but a rustling behind him gave him pause.

Something was in the sleigh. Tensing, Korreth twisted around, just in time to see a small figure pop up from the back.

"Surprise, Papa!" a little male exclaimed, lifting his arms.

"Aeryx!" Korreth barked, doing his best to shield Zira, who, from the feeling and sounds of it, was rushing to make herself decent.

"I mean… BOO!" Aeryx giggled, leaning over the railing of the sleigh. "Did I scare you and your friend?"

Korreth blinked. How had he not seen his son hiding in the sleigh?

6

ZIRA

Papa? *Papa?* Korreth had a son? Aeryx was his *son*. Zira hadn't known who Korreth had wanted Major Enox to relay the goodbye message to. It could have been a father, a brother, a friend, a male lover. But this, this meant there was another female, not just any female though, but one whom Korreth was serious with if they'd had a child. It would most likely be his *mate*.

Zira jumped to her feet and adjusted her pants, her thoughts lingering on where Korreth's hand had just been. Between her legs, his fingers circling her center, and Morozko's teeth, how he'd made her moan. The burning and blissful sensations she'd felt only moments ago had turned as cold as the ivory snow around her.

Swallowing thickly, she took a step away from Korreth.

"I can explain," he rushed the words out, grasping for her wrist.

Zira yanked her arm from his fingertips and slapped him across his chiseled face, the sound echoing throughout the mortal world's winter forest. A mixture of emotions played across his face and she didn't care. "You have a *child*," she seethed through gritted teeth. "Another female who is more than a lover. I don't get in the middle of things of that nature."

"My mother's dead," a small voice said beside her —Aeryx.

Zira whirled around to face the young male, his brows furrowed. She hadn't heard Aeryx approach them, hadn't seen him come out of the sleigh. Then the words struck her in the chest of what the child had just whispered. *Dead.* Her eyes widened as she peered up at Korreth, his wavy hair blowing around his face from the frigid wind.

An emotion formed in his gaze, crestfallen, as he rubbed at his reddened cheek. "Just give me a moment." His tone was gentle as though he was apologizing when she'd been the one who had slapped him.

Zira nodded, taking another deep swallow. Her hand stung from her slap, and she wished she could take it back. His wife? Lover? Mate? Whatever she'd been to Korreth, she was dead. Zira's lover was gone too, but she hadn't mothered a child with Vron. She couldn't begin to imagine what that would be like, if she'd been left alone with a child and her lover gone. She would have survived it, but it would have hurt a thousand times more knowing he would have been missing out on their child.

Korreth bent forward and easily lifted his son in his arms. Aeryx wore a similar black and red uniform to Korreth's, only it was loose on his thin frame. She'd never seen a child wearing a warrior's uniform before.

"Papa, I missed you." Aeryx grinned, wrapping his gangly arms around Korreth. Zira's chest swelled at the loving sight of father and son. Small obsidian horns, still nubs, poked out from between Aeryx's short brown curls, his hair matching his father's. Except his eyes were a darker hue, which he must have inherited from his mother. How had his mother died? Childbirth? Or something worse? Like what Zira had faced?

Korreth's booted feet sloshed through the snow, the only sound around them besides a few chirping birds and the wind rustling the branches. He sat his son in the front seat of the sleigh, the black leather creaking as the child nestled into the soft cushion. Pulling up a folded blanket from the back, Korreth opened and spread the thick fur across Aeryx's lap. He then fished out a piece of fruit from his pack and handed it to him.

Zira shifted from one foot to the other, feeling out of place, unsure of what she should do or say when Korreth turned and walked back toward her. He gripped his neck once more, seeming not as confident for the first time.

"I'm sorry." He shrugged, stopping in front of her, his ice-blue eyes meeting hers. "I don't know what to say."

"No, I'm sorry." She took a step toward him. "I should have let you speak before deciding if I should slap you or not."

A smile played at the edges of his lips. "It was a good slap, wild cat. I know we haven't known each other long, but before things escalated between us, I should have told you about Aeryx. I don't usually do things like this. My son, being a captain—those have been my focus these past years."

"How did his…" Zira bit her lip, not sure if she should ask just yet.

"Mother die?" He scowled, his expression hardening while he studied the branches above them. "Changelings. One of the reasons I continue doing what I do. Two years ago, while Orna was at home, I went to the forest to do my usual training routine. Aeryx was with me that day. He was supposed to have been at home with his mother, yet he tends to follow me wherever I go. He's only six years old, but since the day he could speak, his dream has always been to be a warrior. It's why Major Enox's wife makes him the uniforms in his size."

Zira glanced over at Aeryx, who was eating his apple and leaning over the sleigh, playing with Dral's tail. She couldn't imagine this innocent child one day being a warrior, beating a changeling, then shoving the evil thing into the furnace. But perhaps her villagers would have said the same thing about her and every other krampi when they were younger. One didn't yearn to do this because it was enjoyable—although she'd found pleasure in listening to the changeling die in the furnace—but it was *necessary*.

"Anyway," Korreth continued, "while we were out in the forest, a changeling came inside our home and murdered Orna. The same way they do with all their victims. I should have been there."

"It's not your fault. And if Aeryx hadn't followed you, he would have been dead too..." Zira looked one more time at the child, a sinking emotion stirring within her as she thought about a changeling slashing Aeryx's chest open, tearing him apart, eating his lungs. They had to be stopped.

"I think about it every day, wondering what would have happened if he hadn't followed me." Korreth took a deep breath, changing the subject. "I'm sorry he had to see us like that."

Zira didn't think he'd seen much. They'd both still had their clothing on, and Korreth's body had been covering hers.

Then another unpleasant feeling washed over her, and she pursed her lips. "Do you regret it? Touching me?"

He tucked a lock of hair that had fallen out from her braid behind her ear, then leaned forward, his lips brushing her neck as he spoke. "I only regret that we didn't get to do more."

The deliciousness of his hot breath, his lips, against her flesh sent a shiver through her, a rush of heat coursing within her veins. Zira smiled, her heart quickening. "How about—"

"Papa! Come look!" Aeryx squealed, causing Zira to inch back from Korreth's closeness.

Her gaze found Dral kicking at the snow while licking Aeryx's apple with his long tongue. Zira smiled as Aeryx pressed the rest of his apple into Dral's mouth.

"Make sure you eat enough to fill your belly," Korreth said. "Grab another and don't share this one."

"Has he been staying in one of the barracks?" Zira asked. She hadn't seen him when she'd gone into Korreth's room the other day.

"He's been staying with my cousin Efraun the past few weeks while we concentrated on the new nest of changelings. Aeryx would be safer outside of the barracks since there is always a chance for a changeling attack where we are."

"Should we take him home now?" They weren't far from the portal, and it wouldn't take long to bring him back.

"No." Korreth crossed his arms and shook his head. "Aeryx got himself into this. He's told me on several occasions that he wants to stay and be a warrior. He needs to understand the repercussions for his actions."

Zira's lips parted, a look of horror crossing her face. "But, he's a child."

"He's a child, yet he can defend himself. Aeryx can use

his hypnosis already, so he can influence a human. Not only that, he has learned that nowhere is entirely safe. So if we brought him back, it would only put him into hiding again instead of learning more about what he will one day face. He's by my side, and I will let nothing, *no one*, touch a single hair on his body. I would never put him in serious danger. It's one changeling we must retrieve. Not an entire nest."

Zira mulled it over, wondering if her family had known how to defend themselves better, would they have still been alive? In the past, she had always been the one to shield her sisters, save them when others were bothering them. If only Zira had taught them how to fight back then instead of always being their rescuer…

"I'll keep an eye on him too," Zira promised. "I can teach him how to guard himself."

"Let me show you something." Korreth smiled wide for the first time. Beautiful. Brilliant. She wanted to run her fingers across the curve of his shapely lips. He then turned to his son and motioned him with a finger. "Come here, Aeryx. I want you to properly meet Zira."

Aeryx grinned and took a bite of another piece of fruit he'd scavenged. He tossed it to Dral, who easily caught it in between his sharp teeth before Aeryx hopped from the sleigh.

Korreth placed a hand on his son's arm and gestured toward her. "This is Zira. Show her what you can do."

Aeryx freed a hidden dagger from behind his back faster than any warrior she'd ever seen, then thrust it forward so it was a hair's breadth from touching her chest. He then returned the weapon to its sheath and bowed his head. "I will protect you, Zira."

Her brows lifted and Korreth chuckled. Aeryx's voice had

held a strong amount of confidence for such a small child. In that moment, he appeared almost a mirror image of his father. Only, mischief sparkled within his dark eyes, and the tilt of his lips hinted at a more challenging side of him. He was adorable.

"That you will." Korreth patted his son's shoulder. "But you will stay close to our side and listen to us. A warrior always follows a captain's orders. Can you do that?"

"Yes, sir." Aeryx nodded, straightening to full height. "When are we leaving?"

"We have to wait until later tonight," Zira said, peering up at the star-speckled night sky. "How about we sit here for now and you tell me more about you?"

Aeryx took a seat in the snow and shifted closer to Zira after she sank down. "So you're my papa's warrior? Not a friend?"

She snuck a glance at Korreth and smiled. "Am I his friend? I haven't known him too long, but from what I do know, I believe we're well on our way."

Aeryx cocked his head. "It doesn't take long to make a friend. I know right away if I like someone. And that's if they want to play hide and seek. Can we play now?"

"Aeryx…" Korreth drawled in a deep tone, shaking his head.

"Yes, Papa?" His chin tilted up as he peered at his father. "It will only be right here. I promise I won't go too far."

"Only if Zira wants to. She's rather remarkable at climbing trees and hiding there." A light chuckle escaped Korreth, and he cleared his throat.

It had been so long since she'd done anything like this for fun. She studied Aeryx's wide eyes, his hopeful expression.

After midnight, they would be doing a much darker deed, so for now, it would be a good distraction for the three of them. Until they had to face what they'd come here to do.

"If I can count first. I would like to have the pleasure of searching for your father this time." Zira laughed, remembering just a few days ago when they'd done this in the forest, when she'd fallen from the tree on top of his hard body.

"Count to a hundred and no peeking," Aeryx instructed and darted to a nearby tree covered in icicles.

"Closing my eyes now." She turned around and started counting but not before she felt the soft featherlight touch of Korreth's calloused fingers against hers.

"Thank you for this," he whispered in her ear.

7

KORRETH

The wind carried the scent of pine and the melodic sound of Aeryx's laughter with it as he hid several trees away from Korreth. From the distance, the train wailed, reminding them that this wasn't Frosteria's woodlands, it was the mortal realm. He smiled as he hid behind the thick trunk. He hadn't taken care to cover his tracks because he wanted Zira to find him sooner. A complex emotion speared through his chest as Aeryx had beamed up at her with pride. Both confusing and heartwarming, for Korreth didn't want just *anyone* in his son's life, but Zira was his fated mate. She was a stranger to them both, which made the entire situation complicated.

And she didn't even fucking feel it.

Korreth closed his eyes and leaned the back of his head against the trunk. His horns grazed the bark and caused a sprinkling of snow to dust his face. He wasn't familiar with how the bond worked, outside of what was passed between krampi in talk. Only that the pull was unmistakable. The steady thrum, the yearning to claim, to ensure no other would dare to possess any piece of Zira. It was a constant urge so strong that he could nearly detect where Zira was at any given moment.

It was fucking torturous.

He turned his head to the side as the sound of snow crunching beneath boots drew nearer. The footfall was too heavy to belong to Aeryx, which meant Zira was approaching. He did his best to shutter his expression before she came upon him. Korreth only assumed he looked as if he were ready to devour her, and fuck if he didn't want to.

"Half-ass job, Captain," Zira teased as she rounded the corner and glanced up at him.

Korreth grinned, his voice coming out rougher than usual. "Maybe I *wanted* to be found." He lifted a hand and toyed with one of the loose locks of her hair. It was like silk between his fingertips, and he wanted to grip it tighter, let his tongue lick the seam of her lips, then taste, slowly, all of her. But then he knew he needed to talk to her about his past. "Zira—" he cut himself off, lowering his eyes. "I need to tell you more about Orna."

Zira lifted her hands, shaking her head. "No, you don't have to." She pressed her fingers into the leather of his jacket, as if entertaining the idea of wrapping her arms around his neck.

He wished she would.

"I want to." When he spoke, she dipped her head down, but Korreth used his forefinger to tilt it back. "Orna was a friend since childhood and no more. We were careless, and she conceived Aeryx, but never did we want more than friendship. We were partners on missions and when frustration or boredom settled in, we fucked. I did love her, but as a friend and no more. Orna felt the same." He shrugged a shoulder. "She was never my wife and certainly not my mate. Although we lived with one another, we had an understanding." Korreth drew his head back so he could get a better look at Zira's expression.

She stared up at him with her impossibly dark eyes, searching his face, but other than that, her expression was unreadable.

"The understanding was that we'd raise Aeryx together, but were free to do as we pleased. I focused on Aeryx, and my duties as captain." When Korreth finished speaking, Zira's eyes dropped to his neck, as if not believing him. Not that he could blame her. He reached up and peeled the fur lined neck of his coat down to reveal where a mark should be, but there was nothing.

"I would not lie to you, wild cat." The tips of her nails skimmed the spot, then traced toward his ear. While it was a simple gesture, it ignited an inferno in his veins, sending a shiver through him and a deep heat straight to his length.

"Zira," he groaned her name and dipped his head forward to claim her lips. While his arms enveloped her, she grew pliant, melding against his hips. He dragged his hands up her back, to thread in her hair as his tongue plunged into the depths of her mouth.

"Can't find me!" Aeryx's voice called out from a cluster of trees not far off.

Korreth reluctantly drew away from Zira, the sound of his son's voice sobering him. She looked up at him with her kiss-swollen lips, tempting him to continue. As much as he wanted to pin Zira against the tree and let her ride him until they both came, it wasn't the time. Korreth was patient and there was no need to rush. The last thing he wanted was to chase Zira off before she even felt the tug of the bond.

How did one bring up the discussion prematurely, amidst a mission, with his child present?

Fuck.

"We should probably track Aeryx down." His voice came out roughly.

Zira cleared her throat and stepped back. "I did promise I'd play."

"You can't very well disappoint the child." He cocked his head and offered a small smile.

She stared up at the canopy of trees, sighing heavily before looking at him. "We're not done here."

"No, we've hardly *started* here." The smile that played at his lips slowly turned into a challenging smirk. Korreth's heart hammered in his chest and his length strained against his pants, but the promise of more time with Zira, and that she *wanted* it, made his desire unbearable.

Then she'd have to feel the pull, wouldn't she? Korreth's gaze shifted to glance over her head, and he concealed the frown that threatened to rumple his brow.

"Let's find that little demon." Korreth chuckled.

For an hour, Aeryx made them endure hide and seek, until finally Korreth ordered him to sleep. The mission was fast approaching and Aeryx couldn't be tired while hunting down changelings. The reasoning appealed to Aeryx, and he snuggled up on the sleigh's front seat, burrowing himself as much as he could against the soft leather cushions.

Even though he wouldn't be cold, since krampi could endure winter's bite, Korreth grabbed a blanket from the back and draped it over his son for comfort's sake.

Moving away from the sleigh, Korreth sat on a fallen log and Zira joined him. Even though Korreth was wide awake, his mind running steadily, a certain tiredness crept inside of him. It had nothing to do with sleep and everything to do with wanting to drown out the pulse of yearning. When he closed his eyes, even for the briefest moment, Zira invaded every one of his senses. His nose, his ears, and as her knee knocked into his, his skin. She'd been watching as he tended to his son, but hadn't spoken a word since their game had finished.

"He's adorable." Zira peered back over at Aeryx and smiled.

Korreth shook his head. "When he isn't disobeying me, he has his moments. He's a willful child, but he'll serve well one day."

Zira's eyebrows knitted together as her gaze slid back to his. She studied him closely, her plump lips twisting into a teasing smirk. "I imagine he gets that from you."

He snorted, but considered her words. Aeryx was only half of him, yet he saw so much of himself in his son, except for his rebellious streak. That was all Aeryx's mother. Orna bent the rules on more than one occasion, which meant Korreth had to clean up her messes along the way. "I suppose he had to inherit something from me."

When quiet settled between them, allowing the palpable tension to simmer, Korreth focused on the ice-covered ground. "We'll be moving out in an hour or so. If you can, get a quick sleep in."

Zira's eyes narrowed, as if she were about to argue, but

then she stood and quietly retrieved her bedroll from the sleigh. When she returned to where Korreth sat, she knelt before him. And he couldn't help but imagine her slowly drawing down his pants, her perfect lips around his cock, sucking, pumping, her tongue gliding up and down. *Korreth, get a fucking grip!* He'd never been this filled with lust in his life–it had to be the bond. Or perhaps it was just her. Those sinfully plump lips, the taunting glint in her eyes, and those curves he'd come to know through sparring.

"What about you? Don't you need sleep?" She unfolded the bedroll, smoothing it out before she sprawled out on her stomach, elbows propped up and palms cupping her chin.

Korreth leaned forward on the log and reached out as if he was about to stroke her cheek, but instead he poked her nose. "I won't be sleeping any time soon. I have enough thoughts to keep me wide awake."

"In that case, do you need to run off to the privy?" Zira snorted, then rolled onto her side. "All right. I'll let you suffer in silence. Just don't let the big bads of the forest snack on me while I sleep."

"That won't happen, wild cat," he said, his voice low. "Because the only one snacking on you will be me."

Aside from the blaring of a horn in the distance, and the sound of sirens wailing, silence settled over the clearing. Or as silent as the mortal realm could be. Compared to Frosteria, it was a loud world where true quiet seldom fell.

Korreth was uncertain if Zira had truly fallen asleep, or if she remained still simply because of the tension that had grown between them, one neither could do a thing about, not while Aeryx was present. It was neither here nor there, because Zira didn't stir for the next two hours, not until he crept up next to her and gently shook her shoulder.

"Zira," he whispered. "It's time to go." Korreth drew back just as Zira bolted forward, and if he hadn't moved, her forehead would've connected with his. "Roll everything up while I wake Aeryx." He rose to full height and sauntered toward the sleigh, jostling his son's arm lightly. "Time to go, little warrior."

He grinned as Aeryx sat up, his wavy hair tangling in the nubs on his head. "Time to make that changeling pay." Aeryx's words didn't surprise him. He'd grown up knowing exactly what the demons were capable of, and what they had done to his mother.

Korreth turned his head to the side as Zira approached from behind.

"What now, Captain?" She peered up at him, arching a brow in question.

Korreth stepped into the sleigh and helped his son climb into the back. "Now we drive the sleigh as close to town as possible without entering the streets. We'll have to walk the rest of the way since we'll draw too much attention with our entire ensemble."

Zira tossed her pack into the back and walked around to the other side of the sleigh. She smirked at Aeryx. "Ready to fight?"

He beamed at her, patting his coat pocket where his knife lay hidden. "I am!"

Korreth chuckled. His son was capable, albeit on the young side, but it didn't mean Aeryx lacked ferocity. He took to the training routines as if he'd practiced in Orna's womb. "Let's hope so."

Once everyone was settled, he barked a command to Dral, who jolted forward into a steady trot. Korreth dipped his hand into his jacket, pulling the stone out as he directed Dral into the northern direction.

In a few minutes, they were out in the open again, dashing through the snow alongside the train tracks. The moon hung high in the sky, full and bright, lighting the way for them. Ice and snow glittered brightly, illuminating their way further as the sleigh carried them downhill, toward the center of town.

While the mission was at the forefront of Korreth's mind, Zira sidled closer to him than before. There were always risks with missions, especially with changelings. They tended to be unpredictable, violent and aimed to kill, not subdue. With Zira and Aeryx accompanying him, the need to protect what belonged to Korreth rose.

A little while later, they'd arrived at the edge of town, the street lights overpowered the moon's glow. It'd be difficult to remain under cover, which was why Korreth pressed for them to wait until later.

Dral halted and shook his head, the lights glinting off his ivory antlers. "Aeryx, I'll carry you on my back until we're where we need to be." Korreth slid from the sleigh and reached into the back. He tugged his whip out and attached it to his hip, then drew out long daggers and secured them to the sheaths at his side. Their goal wasn't to kill the changeling, because if they did, the mortal child would die.

"Grab your weapons, Zira." Korreth demanded, then spun on his heel, waiting for Aeryx to leap at his back. "Let's try to make this quick. We must stay in the shadows as much as we can." He stepped forward, his thumb running along the glowing stone.

The mortal settlement was far more congested than he'd expected. House nearly sat on top of house and their yards were miniscule compared to the expansive land each krampi possessed. Decorations littered their property and even clung to the houses themselves. He didn't understand the thought process behind such foolish things, but that was neither here nor there.

Korreth wound his way down the road, sticking to the minimal amount of trees, and whatever cover nature offered them. As he continued down the way, zigzagging through the darkest part of the community, his eyes remained locked on the stone. It started pulsing so strongly, glowing a vibrant blue, that he knew they were at the right home.

Red and white candy canes lined the driveway, leading toward the front entrance. The home itself was larger than most krampi dwellings, and far taller, too. Short shrubs lined a small garden in front of the porch, also decorated in blinking lights. Despite the shrubbery, and browned foliage, there were scarcely any trees, which meant less coverage for them. They were more vulnerable.

Korreth sniffed the air—he didn't *smell* any canines on the premises, but that didn't mean there wasn't one hiding in the depths of the house.

Carefully, he let Aeryx down and signaled to Zira.

"Swiftly and quietly as possible." He dragged a hand down his face, glancing up at one of the second-floor windows. "The key is to not alert the parents," he said wryly. "It isn't so easy when the changelings fight back."

Zira's eyebrows drew inward, but she nodded. "Do we knock them out if they wake up?"

Korreth choked on a laugh. The sincerity in her tone and

the puzzlement on her face was enough to send him into a silent fit of laughter. "Please, whatever you do, don't knock the parents out. Be quick on your feet, evade them, jump out a window…"

Her sheepish expression turned mildly disappointed.

"Mortals are delicate, wild cat. You can't go around knocking them out," he hissed through laughter. "If we're caught, they could alert other mortals, and you see how close we are to neighboring houses. Remember, they don't see us as we are, but as monsters."

Zira rolled her eyes. "All right. I heard you the first time." She glanced down at Aeryx. "What about this warrior?"

"Aeryx, hide in the bushes. We'll need you down here if things go awry, all right?" Korreth tilted his head and Aeryx nodded, closing his fist on his chest before bowing his head, then scurried off into the bushes, hiding as if they were playing a game.

Zira closed the distance between them. "How are we getting in?"

Korreth squinted and pointed up at the nearest window. "It's cracked. We'll go in through there—it's easier this way. Sometimes we must rouse the mortals first, so we can enter the house. It's never ideal, because as you can guess, things go awry. Which is why we must erase their memories and hypnotize them." The way the porch was constructed, it made it easy to climb the railing, to the roof, to the window. Far easier than a tree.

He stepped toward the porch and proceeded to climb upward. Once on the roof, he waited for Zira and yanked her up, before he continued to the window. Fortunately, it was the room they needed. The shell of the mortal girl slept peacefully, but within, the demon waited, and it wouldn't be long before it sensed the krampi. Still, as she slept, her ash-blonde hair hid most of her cherubic face. She looked close to Aeryx's age, perhaps a year younger. The girl's turned-up nose pressed into her fist and she frowned amidst her slumber, which prompted the question of whether the mortals fought against the hold the changelings had on them.

Korreth motioned to the next window and arched a brow in question. *Parents?* Zira, understanding his question, nodded. If things became too heated, they'd have a few precious moments to get the changeling out of the house before the parents swept into the room.

He leaned down, slipping his fingers under the screen to pop it off. Korreth caught the frame, then placed it down. Without the screen, he was free to slide the window up and despite the bulk of his jacket, he fit through with ease.

Just as his boot connected with the hardwood floor, the girl's eyes bolted open. They flashed a cat-like yellow before returning to their natural hue of dark green. The changeling was *awake*.

"Shit." Korreth launched forward as the changeling sprung from the bed. The creature's shoulders curled inward and its back arched as it clambered up the wall, digging its claws into the soft blue wallpaper. A hiss escaped from the changeling's mouth.

Zira remained half in the window and Korreth motioned for her to stay put. He then crossed the room in two strides and shut the door. He stood in front of the creature, barring the only other exit.

"Give it up, you wretched fuck." Korreth seethed, reaching for his whip. At once, the changeling shuddered in a mixture of fear and anger. The demon swiped at the air, hissing, then the imposter's mouth opened wide, too wide to be natural, and an ear-piercing shriek rang out. It caused Korreth's ears to pop, but he remained focused. Time was ticking away, the parents would no doubt be awakening now.

Unraveling the whip, Korreth readied it, but the changeling darted for the window, toward Zira. *Oh, fuck no.* Just before the demon collided with Zira, Korreth cracked the whip, and the leather coiled around its neck. With a firm yank, he pulled the changeling back. As the demon writhed, the whip slackened, and Zira, losing herself in the moment, barreled for the creature, leaving the window unguarded.

Caught between wanting to shield Zira and wanting to stop the demon from escaping, he opted to block the window.

Zira cried out and fell to the side, but wasn't quick enough in her recovery to grab the changeling. Korreth was ready as it launched itself at him with all fours. Enough force connected with him that he flew backward, out the window and tumbled down onto the roof.

Swiftly, he was up on his feet just as the demon sprung forward with a growl. Korreth tried to right himself but lost his balance. The air whooshed by his face as he fell, his grip never loosening on the changeling. The frozen ground ripped the breath from his lungs as his back struck it. A wheeze escaped his lips, but his grip on the changeling only tightened, unwilling to relinquish the demon.

"Korreth!" Zira clambered down, but not before the changeling twisted in his grasp and tore one of the blades free from his hip.

Just like Korreth predicted, the shrieking changeling, added with the commotion of the struggle, alerted the mortals.

He readied for the bite of a blade as his arm tightened around the changeling's waist. Korreth's free arm came up to grab the dagger, but the writhing figure was hard to keep pinned.

Zira was nearly to them, when a loud *smack* sounded and the changeling grew limp against Korreth's body.

Aeryx stood with a darkened candy cane decoration in his grasp and shrugged. "I got it," he proclaimed and regarded Zira, who grinned at him.

Pride swelled within Korreth's chest. "You did well." He turned his gaze to Zira. "Grab the demon," Korreth ordered. "We need to tie it up." He peered up at the window, to find the parents of the girl staring down at them in horror.

To the mortal eye, they saw creatures taller than an average man, with fur covering their bodies, cloven hooves and a long, tufted tail. As if the sight wasn't enough to undo the soundest mind, they saw four pairs of fangs protruding from their mouths, with a tongue that was far too long to remain inside, and white eyes rimmed with red. Their noses were gnarled and dipped down toward the bottom fangs, and on top of their heads rested four, twisting horns.

Long ago, they didn't always wipe the memories of the mortals. They'd allow them to keep their experience as a cautionary tale, but as time went on, the humans grew more fragile, and it became necessary. However, it was how the tale of Krampus came to be, and how it was only naughty children who were hauled away.

A scream erupted from the dark-haired woman, and she tried to shove her husband away, but he remained rooted in place, frozen. "What is that?" the father shouted.

Zira pulled the changeling off him and he sat up, using his

whip to quickly bind the small demon's hands and feet together.

The mortal parents' hysteria then unfolded. "What are you doing to my daughter?" The woman's voice turned shrill.

"Time to go, and *now*. I cannot afford to wipe the memory of every mortal on this drive." Korreth waited until both parents were running toward them. He held his hand outright and a blue wave of magic rose from his palm, then blasted toward them. The parents stood in a daze, seeing and yet not. They twitched, as though fighting to bring their child back home. But a mortal could never win against krampi magic. Their muscles stopped jerking, and they slowly turned around, walking back inside.

Come morning, they'd frantically search for their daughter. But not until then.

The neighboring home's lights turned on, indicating they'd been roused. "We need to go." Korreth picked up the changeling while Zira lifted Aeryx onto her back before hauling ass across the pavement, toward the edge of the forest.

They needed to get the changeling back to Frosteria so they could return the child before dawn.

8

ZIRA

The changeling in Zira's arms hadn't stirred, not once. Not as she, Korreth, and Aeryx walked, not as they sat in the sleigh, and not as they took off.

She yearned to rip the vicious creature straight from inside the child's body, but it couldn't be done that way. Instead, they would have to beat the changeling out of the human, then set flames to the demon. She thought about the one that burned the other day, its screams, its smell.

"Will the child feel anything?" Zira asked as a horrible thought entered her mind. She wanted the human free, but she didn't want the little girl hidden somewhere in this body to feel the pain of the whip.

"No," Korreth said, reclining back in the seat, reins in his hands. "As soon as the monster is out of the human, any wounds vanish. The child will feel nothing before nor after."

Zira relaxed at those words and focused on Dral's bobbing head as he dashed through the snow, his hooves pummeling the earth, galloping faster than he ever had, even while pulling the heavy sleigh.

Aeryx shifted behind her, craning his neck over her shoulder to look at the changeling. He peered at its bound arms and legs while lingering in the back of the sleigh. Korreth hadn't wanted his son in the front in case the changeling woke and became volatile. Zira had also wanted to be the one to hold the demon if it did stir.

"She has pretty hair," Aeryx said, observing the ash-blonde locks. The child appeared to be the same age as Aeryx with a sprinkle of freckles across her nose.

Korreth arched a brow and studied his son. "Do not think of them as anything besides monsters. You can talk about her hair afterward. The moment you think of them as human, it can be a weakness. We know to save the human, but for now, that is all."

Aeryx frowned, seeming to mull his father's words over before finally nodding. "I understand that, Papa."

Some may consider it harsh to think that way, but Korreth was right. After seeing her village destroyed by the cruel crea-tures, it was the only thing to do.

Before the sleigh, the portal flickered a silvery hue, small ivory flecks shimmering, and bright blue flames surrounded its outer edges. A light sizzle, like snow falling, sounded while Dral pulled them through the barrier and back into Fros-teria. As though recognizing that the changeling was returning home, its eyes burst open and it lurched forward, squealing an ugly shrill noise. Even with its arms and legs tied, and its shell being that of a small child, the demon's strength was over-powering.

When Zira struggled to keep her grip on the creature, Korreth dropped the reins and took the changeling from her arms, then hauled it into his lap. The captain's face reddened while the demon thrashed. As Zira moved to help, the creature whirled around and drove its teeth into Korreth's shoulder, tearing through his jacket. Razor sharp teeth protruded from the mortal child's mouth, not belonging to her, but the changeling.

"You little fucker," Korreth seethed, tearing the changeling back. Zira jolted forward, pinning its shoulders down to the cushion.

"Papa!" Aeryx threw a leg over the back of the seat.

"Stay back," Zira shouted to Korreth's son. She knew he wanted to fight, but he was still too young, regardless of how good a little warrior he may be.

"Aeryx, just keep your weapon ready," Korreth instructed while holding down the changeling by its knobby knees.

The creature's wails pierced the air, making it feel as though Zira's eardrums would shatter. She gritted her teeth, flicking her gaze around the wintry trees, searching for other enemies who may have heard the changeling's call. But nothing came out besides a few spotted deer.

Up ahead, the barracks came into view, and thick gray smoke curled toward the sky from the area. Before she could worry that something had caught fire, the scent of burning changeling flesh struck her nose, signaling that some of the other warriors must have already found their prizes.

Dral circled around the fortress, coming to a slower pace as the snow lessened. He drew to a complete stop not too far from several warriors and trainees. They stood before the towering furnace, one set finishing up their duty while the other duo went up the stairs to toss a changeling into the burning flames. A high-pitched shriek sounded after they slammed the furnace door shut. A child rested in each of the trainees' arms, appearing to be asleep, whole. Zira sighed in relief.

Korreth glanced at Zira, his voice tight as he spoke. "I'll get the changeling in the snow and remove its binds. We can't leave the demon tied or it won't be able to leave the body. Grab a whip from the back and save the child." He then turned to Aeryx, who studied the situation with wide eyes. "Stay here, but be prepared."

Aeryx nodded and lifted one of his daggers, the moon's glow glinting off its sharp blade.

Zira pursed her lips, watching Korreth's straining muscles flex as he took the writhing changeling into the snow, tossing the evil thing to the ground. Quickly, she snatched a long whip covered in blue ice spikes from the back of the sleigh. When she'd seen Korreth do this before, she'd wanted badly to use the weapon herself. This was her opportunity now, all while saving a child from its parasite.

Her boots crunched through the snow while she tightened her grip on the whip. She took in the creature that Korreth held down by its back, reminding herself that this wasn't a child. It wasn't an innocent little human girl. It was an evil *fiend*, taking everything from this child, destroying everything in the girl that was good.

"I'm going to cut its bindings, then move out of the way. This will be your challenge, Zira." Korreth paused, his face softening as he looked at her, even though he was dealing with this vicious creature bucking and shaking. "If you need me to intervene, I will. You're not alone in this."

Zira's gaze locked onto those ice-blue eyes of his, and

they somehow grounded her, holding her steady. He was strong, but she was too, especially after what they had both been through in their pasts.

Taking a deep swallow, she held up the whip, waiting for Korreth to make his move. As soon as he pushed off the changeling, he took a knife and sliced through the bindings. When he stepped back, Zira slammed the whip down with a loud crack against the changeling's back. The demon wailed, and yellow smoke drifted into the air from its bloodied flesh. It was already working.

"The more smoke that rises, the closer the changeling is to leaving its shell," Korreth said.

It tried to push from the ground, its body shaking. Zira slammed the whip down before the demon could run, its devious growl echoing around her. Again and *again*, she struck. More and *more*. Perspiration beaded her upper lip and neck, her shoulder aching. She thought the creature might never separate, leaving the child trapped.

Clenching her jaw, Zira brought the whip down once more, and a heavy cloud of dark yellow smoke burst from the body. A shriveled creature, with pale, waxy skin jolted from the child. Tufts of black hair swirled around the top of its head as a breeze wafted by. Zira dove for the changeling and her hand caught its frail leg, but it easily slipped from her grasp. She wouldn't call for Korreth's help. Not yet. She was going to prove she was a warrior and could do this on her own. Nostrils flaring, she barreled after the gnarled creature, pumping her legs harder and harder, until she was close. So close. Then she leaped forward, tackling the demon to the snow.

The changeling's mouth twisted, even with the sinew

sewing the lips mostly shut, it growled lowly, trying to lift its head and roll over. But she held the demon steady, pinning it down.

Heavy footsteps sounded behind her. "Good," Korreth said above her, a smile on his face. "I'll take it from here, then I'll meet you in the sleigh."

Korreth's hands brushed hers as he took the changeling in his grasp, wrapping rope around its wrists and legs once more. Zira's heart pounded while she watched him carry the demon toward the furnace, the adrenaline still rushing through her veins.

"Zira!" Aeryx called. "The girl!"

Morozko's teeth! How could she have forgotten?

The girl rested face down in the snow, the clothing at her back ripped open. Zira knew the wounds were healed, but blue blood still coated the fabric.

Aeryx hurried across the snow to the little girl's side and rolled her over. The human still hadn't stirred as Zira caught up with him. The girl's curls were sprawled across the snow, her skin pale from the cold. Aeryx lightly patted the human's cheek.

"She may not wake right away," Zira said. "Let's get her to the sleigh for now and grab her a blanket." Catching her breath, Zira scooped the girl into her arms—soft sleeping sounds escaped the child as she walked her to the sleigh.

Howls reverberated, and Zira's attention drew to the furnace where Korreth stood at the top of the stairs, the changeling already gone from his arms. The familiar burning scent of the creature's flesh hit her nose once more. It was one less vicious monster, one more child saved. Hopefully, a human life wasn't ruined.

Once he collected a thick blanket from the back of the sleigh, Aeryx crawled into the front seat and Zira sank down beside him. She then wrapped the blanket tightly around the human to give her enough warmth to protect her sensitive flesh.

"What is she going to remember?" Zira asked, peering at the girl. Her parents wouldn't recall the krampi's earlier visit and when the human was returned, it would be as if nothing had ever happened. But would the girl remember the demon sliding into her body, taking over her form? The thought of having one of those creatures slither inside her own form sent a shiver straight to her bones.

"She won't remember," Aeryx said softly. "It will be as if she were in her body the whole time."

Zira wasn't certain how long the changeling had been inside the human, but perhaps not that long since the nest had recently hatched. At least the girl hadn't lost that much time of her life.

As the dying screams of the creature faded to nothing, Korreth spoke to a few lingering warriors before walking to the sleigh.

"I want to be the one to take her home, Papa," Aeryx said when his father approached.

Korreth sighed, running a hand along his jaw. "Aeryx."

"A warrior finishes the job."

"You weren't even supposed to come."

A line settled between the young male's brow, making him appear older than he was. "Mama would have wanted me to save this girl."

Zira's chest tightened at those words, his determination.

He was still a child but had more courage than most of the older krampi from her village.

For the first time, Korreth's shoulders hunched a fraction as he relented. "We'll take you to the edge of the forest and wait for you there, but you're not crossing the barrier to the human world alone just yet.

"Yes, Papa."

Korreth was truly a good father, wanting his son to be independent yet would save him in a heartbeat if provoked. The captain squeezed in beside Zira, the heat of his body pressing into her. Her heart lurched at his touch, the warmth spreading through her. Biting the inside of her cheek, she focused on holding the lower half of the human girl while her upper portion rested in Aeryx's lap.

Dral blew out a huff of air, then took off, not as fast and impatient as before, yet still brisk. The danger was gone, but they still needed to get the girl back home to her parents. After leaving the barracks and traveling for a while through the icy landscape, the barrier slipped into view, its silvery sheen and blue flames flickering as they passed through. A sharp bite from the wind brushed her skin, colder than before.

There was no train barreling down the tracks, but beyond them, the distinct sound of human life vibrated. Like Korreth did the last time, he drove Dral into the cover of the forest.

The girl's eyes peeled open, just as they had when the changeling woke in Frosteria, except she didn't jerk forward, only studied Aeryx with wide eyes.

"What are you?" the girl whispered.

"I'm bringing you back home," Aeryx said, not answering her question.

She blinked, squinting, focusing intensely on Aeryx. "You

look like the Beast in *Beauty and the Beast*, only your fur is darker, and your horns are longer."

Zira furrowed her brow, confused at what this human was speaking of.

"You're not afraid?" Aeryx asked, wrinkling his nose.

She blinked and shook her head. Her gaze shifted to Zira and Korreth, her lips parting.

"You're safe," Zira said, placing a hand to the girl's soft cheek. "You're going to be taken care of and brought back home soon."

"Okay," the human whispered.

Dral pulled them a bit farther until he came to a stop near a large tree with icicles dangling across its bare limbs. Light snow flurries drifted down from the pale blue sky.

"You know what to do once she's home?" Korreth pushed out from the sleigh and walked around to help the girl out.

"Yes, Papa." Aeryx nodded. "It's not far from here."

"You're taking Dral, though. And don't take more than an hour or we'll have to come searching for you."

Aeryx whispered to the girl about having to take her home on the reindeer. Once again instead of being afraid, her eyes opened in wonder while she stared at the beast, as though she believed this all to be a dream. Perhaps it was better this way, even though she would forget it all soon.

Zira watched as Aeryx held the girl's hand and tugged her toward Dral after Korreth finished unhitching the reindeer from the sleigh.

"May I lift you on Dral, little princess?" Korreth asked the girl softly. "He won't harm you and will make sure you stay safe while my son takes you home." Zira couldn't help but smile at this gentle side of the captain.

The girl grinned as Korreth lifted her into the saddle, then Dral lowered his large body so Aeryx could mount him behind the human.

"Remember your lessons, and don't leave Dral's side," Korreth said.

"See you soon, Papa." Aeryx grasped the reins, and Dral walked them through the forest.

"He'll be fine." Korreth scooted closer to Zira. "If I didn't believe so, I wouldn't allow him to go on the short journey. This is the easy part. Then he'll make the girl forget before returning."

The girl hadn't seemed afraid, so it was a shame she would have to forget their brief meeting, but perhaps that was for the better too. It was best for the krampi's protection.

"How's your shoulder?" Zira asked, studying the dried blood on his shirt sleeve.

"It's fine. The demon barely nicked my skin." He paused. "You did good on your first mission."

Zira mulled over everything, her actions finally catching up with her. A bit of melancholy washed over her. "I still wish it didn't have to be that way. But the girl is lucky she only had the changeling in her for a short while."

"Some are inside their hosts for years, sometimes forever."

That was an awful thought. She still wondered where a child was when a changeling took over their body, though. Were they inside seeing everything and unable to do anything? Or were they hidden away in some dark nothingness? Both were horrendous thoughts. "You have a good son," she said to lighten the mood.

"He told me he likes you." Korreth arched a brow.

"Did he?" Zira grinned.

"Yeah."

"What about you?" she whispered, backing him up into the trunk of a tree.

Korreth leaned down, his lips brushing her ear as he purred, "I like you very much, wild cat."

Her chest fluttered at the tickling of his warm breath on her flesh. "Prove it."

Zira released a gasp as he scooped her up and whirled her around, then she was the one backed into the tree. He pressed his strong body into hers until she could feel his hard length pleasantly against her. They didn't have much time before Aeryx returned, so she wasted no time capturing his soft lips with hers. There was no hesitation as he ran the tip of his tongue across the seam of her mouth, then dipped inside. He ground his hips into her as the kiss deepened, their tongues licking, entangling. His hands curved around her ass, drawing her more firmly against him while he continued to roll into her.

Her fingers went to the ties of his pants and unlaced them. Korreth groaned when her fingers dipped inside and traced the velvety skin of his cock. He then growled when she gripped it fiercely and freed him. As she pumped him, he threw his head back, his breathing turning ragged. Their kisses became more wild, frantic.

Korreth took his wonderful mouth from hers, making a whimper escape her. "As much as I want that," he rasped, bringing his lips back to hers in a soft caress, "it's you I want shuddering from pleasure first. I want to taste you, Zira."

With anticipation coursing through her, he unfastened the buttons of Zira's shirt and pulled the fabric back, exposing her breasts. He trailed kisses down her chest, igniting a fire inside her when he brought a hard nipple in between his teeth. He gave it a soothing suck, then circled it with his hot tongue, making the heat within her become a full-blown inferno.

Zira's heart slammed against her sternum, a glorious feeling soaring in her chest as he unlaced her pants and drew them down. She wanted *more*. Needed *more*.

He didn't lay her in the snow though. Instead, he knelt before her, hoisting her onto his shoulders as though she weighed nothing. With her back against the tree, she leaned into it for support, nearly trembling from anticipation of his mouth on her.

They studied each other for a long moment, her gaze fastened to Korreth's. His curls danced around his handsome face, his perfect chiseled features.

A roguish grin played across his lips when he adjusted himself at her core. Zira moaned as he ran his tongue expertly up her center, tasting how ready she was for him. She entwined her fingers in Korreth's hair before gripping his horns, then held them tighter as he circled her, stroked her, made love to her core with his wicked, wicked mouth.

She wanted to taste his seed next, wanted all of him inside her, wanted that tongue to lick every inch of her. Over and over and over *again*.

A cry shot through her as her body jerked, spasmed with ecstasy, delectable euphoria. Then the feeling flowing through her yanked, twisting into something else… pulling… pulling as if a string inside her was yearning to be straightened. It was almost there, not all the way, but she could *feel* it. And then, she knew what it was. Somehow, she was certain.

A rush of fear barreled through her that she hadn't known

Korreth that long, didn't love him yet, but she knew she would. One day, she would love him with her entire heart, her entire essence because… he belonged to her.

The word wouldn't stay trapped in her mouth and spilled out from her lips as a murmur. "Mate."

9

KORRETH

The sweet taste of Zira lingered on his tongue, and the minty scent of her filled his nostrils. Korreth had wanted to do more than use his tongue to bring her to the peak of pleasure, and he'd selfishly wanted her to continue pumping his cock until he came. However, Korreth couldn't deny the urge to taste her any longer, and to feel her shudder around his tongue as he plunged inside her, stroking and drawing out her climax.

He gripped onto Zira's thigh, squeezing it right before she murmured that *word*. His breath paused and his heart nearly stopped as it tumbled from her delicious lips. *What did she just say?* Korreth drew his head back and stared up at her, his brow furrowing in question.

She looked startled, her chest heaving, as Korreth studied her, like she didn't quite comprehend what she'd muttered. He released her thigh and carefully slid her to the ground before he stood. Korreth helped her button her shirt while she adjusted her pants. Then he lifted his hand and brushed his thumb along her bottom lip, his gaze locked on hers.

Heart pounding in his ears, he leaned in closer, her body pressed tightly to his. "What did you say, wild cat?"

"You're my mate," she whispered, her eyes wide. Zira trembled still, whether it was from the fading waves of pleasure or… did he see a hint of fear in her eyes?

"Zira," he said her name softly and trailed his hand from her chin to cup her cheek. "You feel it *now?*" Korreth closed his eyes and rested his forehead against hers. "I will not rush you into anything."

Zira laughed. It was a half-strangled noise, as if she wasn't sure whether she *should* be laughing. "You just had your head between my thighs, Captain. I think we're past formalities."

His lips twisted into a grin and his tongue darted out to wet them, still tasting of her. "True, but I mean I won't press for more than that, if it's what you desire."

She watched as he shifted away from her. "How long have you known?"

What did he tell her, aside from the truth? That he'd known since Major Enox paired them together for training. That every time her body collided with his, it was fucking torture. He'd wanted to kiss and taste every inch of her, bury himself inside of her so he knew every intimate sound she would make when he brought her to pure bliss. He wanted it all.

"Since you arrived at the fortress." He lifted his hand and rested his forearm against the tree above her head. "I thought it was fate playing a cruel trick on me. Fating me to someone who wasn't meant to bond with me." It wouldn't have surprised him, not with how his life had gone in the past decade. Orna dying, losing comrades—it made growing close to anyone difficult, when at any moment they could be ripped from him.

"Oh." Zira's gaze lightened. The fear turned to mirth and a slow smirk curled into a devious smile. "So, all those days with me…"

He lifted his eyebrows and cocked his head. "Was fucking hell? Yeah, that about sums it up." Despite the dry tone, he chuckled, which turned to a low hiss as Zira's hands dipped back into the front of his pants and encircled his throbbing length.

Korreth's eyes drifted shut, but when they opened, he turned his head to the side, half expecting his son to come rushing back. A part of him was uncertain of whether it was too soon for Aeryx to return the mortal by himself, and yet, Korreth trusted his son and knew he'd take the mission seriously.

"No, don't worry about if Aeryx shows up again. I'll keep an eye out, but you deserve to feel pleasure too." Her thumb swirled along his tip, sending a shudder through him. Korreth's better senses told him to wait, but he was tired of waiting, tired of always controlling every emotion.

He inhaled sharply the moment Zira's hand slid down his length, caressing the underside, all the way down to its base. She massaged his flesh, then worked her hand back up, squeezing before that damnable thumb circled his tip again. Korreth's hips bucked, yearning to fill more than just Zira's palms. But as he closed his eyes, he imagined her sprawled on her back, waiting for him to dive into her depths.

He rocked his hips forward, allowing the primal part of himself to let loose. Korreth sucked in uneven breaths, moaning Zira's name while the impending climax blossomed within.

Zira's breath hitched as Korreth trailed his hand to her hip and squeezed. The scent of mint enveloped them, intoxicating him, but he wasn't entirely senseless, he knew he couldn't just fuck her on the ground while Aeryx was bound to return.

"Give in to me, Captain," she purred and caught his lips, letting her tongue dive into his mouth. He groaned as her tongue slid against his, only increasing the fire that burned beneath his skin.

Korreth's eyes slammed shut and his body trembled. He growled when he climaxed, bending forward as he spilled himself into her awaiting hands. Pleasure still zinged through his veins, weakening his muscles for the moment. Korreth felt as though he could tumble over if a gentle breeze brushed across him.

A new intensity hummed inside his veins. While it sated his desire a fraction, it also increased his *need* to mate with her all the more. Judging by Zira's flushed cheeks and the scent of new arousal, she felt the same.

Zira was everything he could ask for in a mate. Capable. Clever. Daring. While they may not have known one another well enough, they had time now.

"We're almost done here, wild cat." He lifted a hand and cupped her cheek, his eyes locked onto hers. "Then, I vow to properly claim you as my mate, and I will show you the importance of endurance training."

She leaned forward and captured his lips, gliding her tongue along his. "We'll see who can't keep up when the time comes."

Korreth took a step back and tucked himself into his pants,

but his eyes never wavered from Zira's. "I accept your challenge." He reached inside his jacket and pulled out a kerchief to wipe her hands clean.

She turned away from him and found a seat in the form of a stump. Now they waited for Aeryx to return.

He looked her over from head to toe, his skin prickling from the heat and desire building already. The drumming in his veins whispered Zira was *his*, and that he must ensure no one took her from him. It was a deep-rooted instinct, Korreth supposed. A way that krampi knew they were compatible, but how could anyone ignore the yearning and the impulse to mate?

Not long after his thought of his son's return, Dral burst through the brush, jumping over a log and into the clearing with a rosy-cheeked Aeryx on his back.

"I returned her, Papa!" Aeryx inclined his head, grinning.

Korreth approached them, patting his son on the leg. "Well done. Did anyone see you?" He lifted a hand, scratching Dral on his rump. "And thank you, Dral, for keeping him safe." The beast stomped the ground impatiently, as if waiting for something else. Korreth turned his attention back to Aeryx.

"Nope! I was sneakier than a changeling."

Zira laughed from her perch on the stump. "That's pretty sneaky."

With the child back in her rightful place, it was time to return to Frosteria and prepare for the next nest of changelings to hatch. Korreth's body seemed to sigh—his shoulders relaxed, and he looked from Zira to Aeryx. There was no use fighting a smile. He reached out and ruffled his son's hair.

"You'll be better than me one day, of that I have no doubt." Korreth wrapped his arms around Aeryx's waist and helped him down from Dral. "Let's get him hitched again so we can go back home." He lifted his hand, scratching along his familiar's furry neck. The beast groaned in delight, shifting his head to poke Korreth with one of his antlers, as if to say *keep going*. "All right, you'll get treats when you're back in the stable."

"I can get him hitched," Zira chimed in as she walked up to Dral, running her fingers along his muzzle. Her lips twitched in a softer smile before her eyes met his. "If that's all right with you, Captain."

Fortunately for him, Aeryx missed the way she'd purred her words. He swallowed roughly and nodded.

"Oh, I'll help, too!" Aeryx stepped up to Dral's head and wound his fingers around the halter, then tugged the reindeer toward the awaiting sleigh.

Korreth motioned for Zira to follow Aeryx. "By all means, take the lead, Aeryx."

She laughed, following his son's instructions. Zira was patient and didn't patronize Aeryx as he told her what to do and the reason behind it.

Although a simple gesture, it warmed Korreth to see the way she interacted with him. That while she wasn't his mother, there was potential for a deep friendship between the two. She could've resented the fact Aeryx wasn't hers, but she didn't, which was a relief.

Once Dral was properly hitched, Korreth made his way into the sleigh. Aeryx tumbled over the front seat and into the back, settling in for the ride. Korreth then pulled a blanket over his son and tucked him in.

When Korreth leaned against the cushion, Zira scooted closer and pressed her shoulder into his.

"Away we go," Korreth said, clucking his tongue to Dral as he summoned the portal. Blue flecks formed first, spitting like sparks from a fire before it opened into a glowing circle. The sleigh jolted forward, then they were through.

Dral's hooves landed on freshly fallen snow that was far more muted than the ice in the mortal realm. He grunted as Korreth directed him down a pathway.

Zira twisted at the waist, peering over her shoulder. "This isn't the way back to the barracks." Confusion laced her tone as she turned to glance up at Korreth.

Unlike the prior path they'd taken, this one was heavily wooded, rather than open tundra. Giant evergreens nearly blocked out the moon's radiance and they clustered together so thickly that a few had grown too near, their limbs wrapping and weaving around one another.

"You're right." A grin tugged the corners of his lips. "I'm on my way to Efraun's dwelling so he can watch Aeryx."

"At this hour?"

"Judging by the moon's position, it's nearly dawn, which means he'll be awake soon."

Korreth found it amusing that she was so fussed about waking Efraun before sunrise. "Nevertheless, even if it wasn't, my younger cousin wouldn't refuse us."

"Well, that must come in handy. But why are we going to your cousin's place?" Zira lifted her brows, waiting expectantly.

She must've thought he had a trick up his sleeve or perhaps an alternate plan, but the truth was, they both deserved some down time. Aeryx was safe, the changeling had been killed, and the human child returned. "There is a place that rivals our magic and can make even the most stoic krampi stare in awe."

When the forest gave way to open land, a wooden cottage came into view. His cousin's home was almost on the outskirts, which often lent him a more eccentric air. Still, his home was safer than the barracks right now.

Winterberry bushes lined the front of the home, and the red berries bobbed in the gentle breeze. Purple crocuses dotted the in-between spaces, their bulbs in full bloom. Smoke billowed from the chimney and the warm glow of candlelight filled the windows in the dwelling. Efraun was awake.

Dral quickened his stride, hauling the sleigh up the small incline, and halted in front of the doorway. They'd hardly come to a stop when the door opened, revealing a shadowed figure.

"Before you say anything… I'll have you know, I knew he was safe with you." Efraun lifted his hand in surrender.

"Is that so?" Korreth drummed his fingers on the iron rail. "I don't buy it. You didn't know where he was."

"Not true," Efraun blurted, and stepped into the light of the moon. "I homed in on his magic and knew exactly where he was." Long, shoulder length hair, the color of tree bark, tumbled to his shoulders, and his eyes were the color of tree sap.

If Efraun didn't possess the ability to track, he would've been in a world of hurt. Cousin or not, if he'd lost Aeryx...

"After he ran off!" Korreth dragged a hand down his face before sliding from his seat. He motioned for Aeryx to hop out. His son bounded across the snow and leaped at the taller male's legs, squeezing them. He earned a ruffling of the hair.

"I'll be back before the next sunset." He lifted a finger, narrowing his eyes. "And this time, don't lose my son."

From the corner of his eye, Korreth could see Zira wave.

Efraun leaned over and picked up Aeryx before walking toward Dral, grinning the moment his gaze locked onto Korreth. "I'll watch over the mite." Efraun lifted his hand and lightly clipped Aeryx on the chin. "We'll try to stay out of trouble."

Korreth snorted. "I don't believe that for a second. However, at least try."

Efraun shook his head, chuckling. "We'll be here!" He turned around and padded back inside the cottage with Aeryx on his hip.

Korreth plopped down beside Zira, and she twisted so her elbow rested on the back of the seat. "So, about this place, Captain… It doesn't pertain to a mission?" she asked, lifting a brow.

"No. As of right now, wild cat, the only mission there is, happens to be showing you one of Frosteria's wonders." The grating sensation of the bond had dulled on the journey to Efraun's, but he still wanted to throw her over his shoulder and lay her down in the forest. There would be another time for that, perhaps when they returned to the fortress, but for now, he wanted to show her one of the most beautiful places in Frosteria.

"Your mission?" Zira's voice raised an octave and a look of incredulity glimmered in her eyes.

"All right. Not the best term to use." He chuckled. "I just want you to see it." Korreth turned away and grabbed the reins, then shot her a playful glance. "I wasn't exaggerating when I said it's beautiful." With a light tap of the leathers,

Dral lurched forward and pulled the sleigh back down the small hill and toward the frozen road.

In the distance, jagged mountain peaks jutted toward the sky like icy daggers yearning to slice open the early morning horizon.

The trees were not as dense as the sleigh continued down the ice road toward the mountains. But it wasn't the mountains they were journeying to—there was a place just before the giant formations that Korreth used to frequent when he was younger with Efraun and Orna.

"Are we there yet?" Zira asked playfully, studying the scene before her.

He tilted his head back, groaning. "Are we going to do this?" He arched a brow, smiling, then turned his attention toward the road again.

As the road grew narrower, the mouth of a cavern came into view. Barbed pieces of ice formed fang-like icicles, giving the appearance that it would swallow any trespasser whole. But as the sleigh approached, nothing shuddered, and no beast came to life.

The runners bit into the ice, producing a soft screech as Dral came to a halt. Korreth slid from his seat and walked to his familiar's head. "I'm not sure how long we'll be inside, and I don't want him just standing here." He spoke as his fingers nimbly undid each leather strap that bound the reindeer to the sleigh.

Korreth brought his fingers under Dral's chin and unbuckled the bridle before sliding it off. "Wait for my call. Until then, my friend," he murmured, placing his palm against the reindeer's forehead. A faint pulse of blue shone beneath his hand and the beast rumbled contentedly. "Off you go."

Dral darted away, churning up ice chunks in his wake.

Entirely alone now, Korreth closed the distance between himself and Zira. "Have you ever been here?" He cocked his head and waved his hand before them.

Zira's brow furrowed and her nose wrinkled. "No, I haven't. I've been to others, but not this particular one."

He smiled at her, then laced his fingers with hers. "Time to change that." Korreth led her inside, and instead of being dark, it was brightly lit. Light, the same hue as the magic they could call on, blazed at the bottom of the cavern and reflected off the shards of ice.

Zira inhaled sharply at his side, but the sight was nothing in comparison to the deepest part of the cave.

"This really isn't like what I've seen." Zira pulled away from him and ran the tip of her finger along a massive icicle hanging from the ceiling.

It was an innocent enough gesture, but after having her hands on his length before, it was enough to undo him.

A ragged breath loosed itself from him. Korreth couldn't control himself any longer. Unceremoniously, he scooped Zira into his arms, and she flailed much like her moniker—a wild cat.

She laughed but ceased her flailing and, instead, looped her arms around his neck. However, Zira's eyes continued to dart around the cave and Korreth didn't blame her. There was so much to take in.

The echo of their existence in the cave was a strange one, deep and melodic as it reverberated and bounced from wall to wall. Korreth turned down a darkened path and Zira's nails skimmed the back of his neck.

His throat bobbed. The feeling of her nails along his skin was making it difficult to concentrate.

"Wait, what's ahead?" Zira whipped her head around to look at him. Her dark eyes were an endless sea of curiosity, tugging at a cord deep within him.

He withheld a shiver that had little to do with the cold. Korreth motioned to the illuminated pool, which offered more light in the darkest part of the cave. "The simple answer? It's a hot spring, but more than that. You can feel the vibration of magic from it." He removed his jacket and tossed it down on the ice.

Zira's attention wasn't on the breathtaking view of the pool—her deep brown eyes were locked on his chest. Despite the thick jacket, the changeling's teeth had punctured through the several layers.

An unreadable expression passed through her eyes. Anger? Frustration? "Let me see what that fucker did." Zira closed the distance between them and pressed her fingers to the torn leather uniform.

When he didn't argue or push her hand away, she started unbuttoning, then she shoved the top aside. Zira brushed his pectoral muscle which sported a new bite mark to add to his collection of scars.

"This is nothing," Korreth murmured lowly.

"It's not *nothing*." She frowned, but he slid a finger beneath her chin and tilted her head back.

"I am alive, Zira." His lips caressed hers in a featherlight kiss and while he hadn't intended for more than that, her arms snaked around his neck, and she pressed herself into him.

She drew in a shaky breath. "But—" Korreth silenced her worries with his lips, allowing his tongue to dance with hers.

His arms secured her against his hips. His cock twitched to life as she rubbed herself against him needily, and the maddening scent of her sex fanned his flames of desire.

Zira shrugged out of her jacket and discarded it on the floor.

With Zira's coat gone, Korreth gained access to her uniform. He stepped back so he could watch as his fingers undid the leathers, and little by little, the flesh he'd yearned to see was exposed. Perfect, creamy breasts sprung free as he peeled her top away and pushed it to the floor.

He dipped his head low, taking her hardening nipple in his mouth to suckle and tease with his tongue.

"I've wanted to touch you since I saw you in your quarters," she breathed the words as her hands roamed over his chest, carefully avoiding the new wound given by the changeling. Her hands left an inferno in their wake. Zira moved lower until her fingers paused at his hips. She knelt before him, unlacing his boots and her own, but when she drew herself up, her fingers tugged his button free, and she shimmied his pants down.

Korreth's length sprung free. Hard and ready to fuck, to claim her as his, but as her damnable quick mouth encircled him, her hands gripping his ass, every muscle in his body tensed. She sucked his tip, drew mind numbing circles around it, then bobbed down, taking him deeper into her mouth.

"Fucking hell, Zira." Korreth rasped and took himself from Zira to shove the remainder of his clothing all the way off. He then knelt on the discarded jackets, looming over her as he panted, "I'm going to enjoy listening to you scream in pleasure." Korreth yanked on her legs so her back hit the floor.

She grinned as he ripped her boots free, then her pants, and when she was entirely bare before him, Korreth dragged his hands down her long legs in a feather light touch.

"I don't want you to be gentle, Captain, I want you to *claim* me."

Korreth captured her lips and the tip of his cock nudged the entrance to her sex. He coated himself in her alluring arousal. "You are mine, Zira." With a quick thrust, he entered her welcoming depths.

Zira cried out, shifting her legs to wrap around his waist, driving him deeper. "Captain."

"No," he groaned. "My name, say my name, wild cat." He withdrew himself, only to slam deeper into her heat. As their skin collided, the sound created a heated melody in the cavern.

"Korreth!" She panted his name, meeting every thrust with a rock of her hips.

He wasn't sure what he'd been expecting as the bond snapped into place, but as an icy-hot sensation snaked through his body, filling him with a frenzy, Korreth assumed that was it.

Zira shoved at his chest, forcing him to rock backward. He slid his arm beneath her and hauled her onto his lap and, in return, garnered a moan from her as she sank down onto him fully.

His eyes traveled along her face, watching as the same lust filled her gaze. Zira's hands settled on his shoulders as she rode him, hard and fast. Her pace was unrelenting, but he matched each downward stroke with an upward thrust.

Korreth wanted to absorb every sound, every touch, but

the buzzing in his veins, in his head, and the frenzied movements of Zira were far too much.

And when he felt as though he could endure no more, her inner walls clamped around him, shuddering. Together they came undone. "Zira," he bellowed, squeezing her hips as he rocked her faster against him.

After the heightened bliss fully washed over them, Korreth rolled onto his back and drew her up to his chest. He glanced down at her, her blonde locks tumbling away from her neck to reveal a newly-formed mark.

At first glance, it looked no more than an odd scar. Silver in appearance, but it sprawled toward her shoulder, like cracked ice. The elaborate design was like a snowflake, where several of its branches extended into smaller ones.

Lazily, she peered up at him and lifted her hand, allowing her fingers to skim what must have been his mark. "Mine," she whispered.

"Only yours." He tugged her so she was on top of him, and his arms encircled her, securing them together. Korreth pressed his lips to hers and although they'd just fucked, he wanted her again. This time, it wouldn't be a frenzy, this time, he'd draw it out until she could take no more.

10

ABOVE ZIRA, THE LIGHT FROM THE HOT SPRING REFLECTED off the ceiling, like stars within a sapphire sky. Her eyelids were heavy. Her body was spent. She'd never been this exhausted while having her heart full at the same time. A warm arm curved around her waist, drawing her closer into his side.

Korreth was a generous lover, tasting her, stroking her, devouring her. He'd made her come and come again, until her body felt like it had burst into countless fragments.

They'd been lying there quietly for a while, catching their breaths, absorbing the beautiful silence between them. But Zira wanted more conversation, whether with their mouths or their bodies.

Propping herself up, she stared into his bright blue eyes and smiled. A lock of his wavy hair was stuck to his face— their bodies had been slicked with sweat from their pleasurable activities.

Grinning, she tucked his hair behind his ear. "Well, Korreth, that was unexpected. I shall say a *good* unexpected, but I shouldn't have been surprised. Not after everything we did in the forest of the human world." Yet, she still was. There were moves and positions that were new to her, bringing a higher level of euphoria.

Drowsily, Korreth's eyebrows lifted, and he smirked at her. "I knew it would be beyond expectations."

"So cocky." She laughed.

He rolled her over until he was nestled between her legs, but this was a different type of feeling as he stared down at her. It wasn't about lust, it wasn't about fulfilling desire, it was about that thing that was blossoming between them. "I want to know everything about you." He brushed the tip of his nose with hers. "What you do in your spare time. What your favorite color is. Anything and everything."

"That would take a while. More than we have time for today, Captain." She ran a finger across his cheek. "But my favorite color is blue."

"Ah, so you were drawn to me because of my eyes. I get it now." He chuckled.

"Yes, if you had green eyes, I would have run far, far away," Zira drawled. She cradled his cheek, taking in each of his strong and handsome features. Korreth closed his eyes as she trailed her digit down his jawline, to his neck. Then he shivered when she traced his mating bond mark with feather light motions. It was still a strange thing, a wonderful thing. She truly believed she was never meant to have a mate and hadn't thought it would feel like this. This perfect.

Under the cave's illumination, everything appeared ethereal—the stalagmites, the columns, the spring, but more than anything there, Korreth did.

She grazed her finger up to one of his horns and he

groaned at the touch. Besides for the length between a male's legs, their horns were just as sensitive and receptive to the brush of a hand. After being with Korreth, Zira realized it was the utmost truth that having large horns meant their cock mirrored them in size. Perhaps even larger.

Zira had never moved this fast with anyone—Leeana had been her childhood friend first, and Vron she'd known for almost as long. But even if the mating bond wasn't there, she believed she would have eventually been drawn to Korreth anyway—once she'd gotten past the stiff exterior he tended to put up. How could she not? Especially after seeing him around his son.

"What now?" she asked.

"That is the question." He kissed her between the brows.

"I'm serious."

With one swift motion, Korreth was off the ground, and she was in his arms. "This." He grinned, cradling her close to his strong chest.

"You have to be clearer than saying *this*." She rolled her eyes.

Chuckling, he buried his nose in her hair. "We should bathe before heading back." Korreth took a step into the spring and light steam rose from its glistening surface.

"I suppose we should," Zira said slowly. She truly did need to clean though, not just from their lovemaking, but from the past couple of days.

He walked her to the middle of the spring, the warm water skimming her skin as he descended farther down into the water. The magic within her stirred at the same time their mating bond shifted. It was as though her magic had become stronger with the addition of the bond, and from what her parents had told her, both lovers would experience this.

As Korreth lowered her into the liquid, her breasts brushed his chest. The spring shimmered even more around them.

Zira's breaths mingled with his before his lips molded to hers in a gentle caress.

"I thought we were supposed to be bathing," she whispered against his mouth.

"I couldn't control myself." He took a step back, his expression shifting into one of authority. "Now, turn around."

Arching a brow, she moved to face the other direction. "I'm waiting for my surprise, Captain."

He then pressed closer until his chest was flush with her back. "I'm going to take care of you."

She thought he meant to take her right there, but when his hands lifted water, and he ran his palms across her flesh, it was a different form of pleasure as he helped wash her. Korreth's movements were as generous as his lovemaking when he wiped the debris from her skin. He then tipped her head back and gently drizzled water through her hair, rinsing it clean as he nipped at her neck and traced her mating bond tenderly with his tongue.

"All clean," he whispered in her ear.

"Your turn," Zira purred, whirling around in his arms. She repeated his motions to every inch of him, each of his scars, and when she got to his length, she made sure to pay extra care there, rubbing and stroking thoroughly.

Korreth's eyes fluttered. "Wild cat," he rasped. "I need you one more time."

"I'm not complaining." Zira released him and her lips

captured his in a fierce kiss. They would need to return to the barracks soon, focus on more of the matters at hand with the changelings. She would fight and fight until the creatures were all gone, wouldn't ever give up, and she would have the perfect captain by her side. In more ways than one.

"You won't be going to the barracks tonight. You'll be staying with me…" His fingers traced the newly-formed mark on her neck, his eyes focused on hers, and Zira found a new warmth inside them. "Major Enox will allow it."

"Oh?" She grinned against his lips. "Would you say that to any other warrior?"

"No, only to my mate." His smile mirrored hers. "But it will be different since Aeryx will be staying with me. That is, if you're okay with that."

Her chest swelled at what she was gaining. A son. A fierce and protective little warrior. "I'm flattered you want me there."

"Good."

"Now, less talking." She drew closer, wrapping her arms around his neck and circling her legs around his narrow hips. He waded through the water, taking her to the smooth wall on the opposite side.

Her lips captured his mouth again, claiming it, but she'd already claimed every part of him, just as he had her. And in that moment, they did nothing except focus on the art of kissing. His fingers dug deliciously into her thighs until they both needed more. With one easy motion, he gradually slid inside her, filling her. Zira arched her back, tightening her legs around him.

Her heart pounded in her chest with something different, new, while his movements were unhurried, slow, gentle as he took his time with her. He flicked his tongue over her lips, and she nipped at his.

And then after each exquisite thrust, each glorious pump, the rush of bliss screamed within her. Specks of water lifted around her as her magic ignited, freezing the moisture midair when she shouted his name.

Korreth quickly followed suit, his body quaking against hers as he released a deep groan. Their chests heaved while they studied one another. He smiled and peered across the hot spring at the frozen water droplets floating in the air.

"You didn't tell me you could do that many at once."

"I didn't have time to show you everything I could make." She let the rush of magic flow through her, shaping the water and freezing it.

Korreth stared at her creation as it rose from the water—an ice horse with wild hair, sharpened teeth, and a muscular body. "Can you make a larger one?" he asked.

"Maybe?" Zira shrugged.

"For Aeryx."

"I can certainly try." She'd only been able to make smaller things in the past, but with how her magic was feeling now, it was possible.

They swam through the warm liquid, back to the other side of the spring. Zira pulled herself out and gripped Korreth's hand to help him out of the water, even though he didn't need it.

He dried her off with his jacket, then she returned the favor by running it up his defined torso, his broad chest, and perfectly shaped backside. Zira handed him back his jacket and got dressed, knowing their time spent in a secluded getaway from the dangers of the world was coming to an end.

As they trekked out of the cave, Korreth let out a loud whistle, echoing across the wintry forest. A strong gust of wind blew past them while they waited for Dral, who broke through the forest in a steady gallop a few moments later.

"I'll hitch him up," Zira said, wanting to continue to get to know Korreth's familiar more. She ran her hand through the reindeer's soft fur when she finished, and he nuzzled her shoulder, seeming to sense the new bond between her and Korreth.

On the way back to Efraun's, she leaned into the captain's chest while his arm wrapped around her waist. He chatted to her mostly about Aeryx, how when his son was at the barracks, he practiced more than any other warrior.

"Tell me something else about you," he said.

"I hate reading," Zira started. "My sisters loved books though, so the rooms in the house were filled with them. After my family's death, I didn't want to go back into the house, so I mostly stayed to the forest. But really, I never wanted to clear the rooms out. I wanted to leave them as they were, as if my sisters and parents would come back." Her chest tightened at the memories of her sisters gathered by the fire while they read and Zira sewed, her mother cooking hot stews, and her father tending the garden.

"After Orna died, I set fire to our house." Korreth exhaled. "It's the opposite of what you did, but both ways are a different sort of healing." Everyone healed differently—there was no right way to move forward.

Dral slowed to a stop, and Zira hadn't been paying enough attention to realize they were already near Efraun's home. His purple crocuses were the brightest color in the garden. Before Korreth hopped out of the sleigh, the door to the cottage opened and Efraun sauntered out. He wore a simple black linen that hung open at the top. Efraun's hair, which had hung free before, was now in several small, knotted braids, lending him a frazzled appearance. Although, his warm easy smile, and the lax way he stood, contradicted the notion.

He was just as good looking as Korreth, and anyone would know they were of the same blood by his chiseled features and strong jaw. Efraun arched a brow when he came to a stop in front of Korreth, his gaze drifting down to his neck that was hidden beneath the jacket. "You just wanted to show her the caverns?"

Korreth shrugged.

Efraun's eyes then fixed on Zira's. "I thought I should properly introduce myself since my cousin hid you away in the sleigh the last time." He bowed at the waist, pounding a fist to his chest. "I'm Efraun."

Korreth cocked his head. "You didn't lose my son again, did you?"

Zira laughed, bowing her head in respect, but the banter between Efraun and Korreth left little room for her to speak.

"Hey, that was only once, and he can defend himself better than I could."

As if hearing he was being discussed, Aeryx flung himself out the door, a big grin on his face. "Papa! Am I coming to the fortress tonight?"

"Yes." Korreth lifted his son into the sleigh between him and Zira when he approached. "Since you helped so well with the mission, you will be training more. If you want to, that is."

"Yes, Papa." Aeryx's eyes brightened as he leaned closer. "But I need to call you captain in front of everyone there, right?"

"Just as a warrior would."

Zira smiled at the cute exchange and Efraun shoved his hands in his pockets, bidding a farewell before heading back inside. Dral took off on a heavy sprint, darting easily through the snow until they arrived at the barracks. Just as when she was here last, thick smoke billowed in the air. More changelings must have been captured by warriors and their recruits. The thought sent a satisfying rush through her.

Once Dral came to a halt, and after Korreth unhitched his familiar, they grabbed their packs out of the back of the sleigh. Zira then started for the building where Korreth's room was, and he pulled her back by the strap of her pack. "This way, wild cat. When I have Aeryx with me, I stay in the Command building."

Zira nodded and followed him and Aeryx toward the building where she'd relaxed by the fire and chatted with Korreth after she'd won the hide and seek challenge. In the wide room, several warriors sat in chairs, drinking out of silver mugs. But Korreth didn't linger and led them down a long hall filled with paintings of mountains and snow-covered trees on the pale walls. He stopped at a door near the end, then fished out a key to unlock it.

Inside was what looked to be a sitting area with a chaise, two chairs, and three doors, which she assumed led to at least two bedrooms. An organized desk took up one corner and a bucket full of toys rested beside it.

Zira removed her pack and jacket, then noticed Aeryx frowning at her. She stilled. It was the first time she'd seen him look at her with a truly displeased expression. Perhaps he thought she was trying to replace his mother.

"What is it?" she asked softly, knowing he'd caught sight of her new mark.

"You're mated to someone." His shoulders slumped. "That means you won't be staying around."

Korreth blew out a breath and knelt in front of his son. "I should have explained this as soon as we picked you up. But Zira isn't someone else's mate—she's mine."

Aeryx cocked his head and wrinkled his nose. "I don't ever want to be mated with someone."

"And why's that?"

Pressing a hand to his chest, appearing older than he was, he released a sigh. "Because I wouldn't get to choose."

Zira understood that, but the mating bond, at least after experiencing it, chose the one who someone would be most compatible with, who they could love fully.

Aeryx then slung his arms around her, squeezing her tight. "But I'm glad the bond chose you."

Her brows shot up and she hugged him back as Korreth stood and watched them with a soft expression.

Zira lowered herself to Aeryx's height, so it was just the two of them. She was still new to him, but she wanted to give a piece of herself to the little warrior. "I know we're recent friends, but I want you to have something." Opening her pack, she pulled out her sisters' small music box and pressed it into his palm. "Any time you feel sad or defeated, listen to its music."

Aeryx wound it up and let the soft melody float through the room. Instead of tears pricking at her eyes at the familiar sound, she smiled. He gently slid the box into his pocket and cupped his hands around her ear so only she could hear while he whispered, "I've always wanted a brother. But a sister would do."

Zira's lips parted as she peered at Korreth, who seemed to be trying to figure out what Aeryx had said. Babies weren't something she wanted any time soon. Pregnancy would slow her down during training, but one day wasn't out of the question.

Aeryx straightened and looked at his father. "What are we doing tomorrow?

"Preparing. More changeling nests will be coming, especially with the recent hatchlings being caught so quickly." Korreth's expression grew serious. "Are you ready, little warrior?"

"Yes, Captain." Aeryx bowed his head. "Can I grab some cocoa from up front?"

"You can have two cups." Korreth kissed the top of Aeryx's head before his son left the room. He turned to Zira, chewing on his lip. "I know you didn't ask for this, any of it."

Cradling his face, she pressed her mouth to his. "I want you. I want it all. I want you to be my captain both in the bedroom and outside of it. And I want to see what each day brings after today."

He drew her close, his arms circling her waist. "Then you should have it all, wild cat. Every bit of it."

TRAVEL BACK TO FROSTERIA . . .

Sometimes, the beauty does claim a beast.

Aeryx is a warrior in Morozko's army, yearning to destroy those who brought ruin to his home. But when duty brings him to the human world, he encounters a problem. An intoxicating problem he wants nothing to do with.

A problem he can't resist.

Noel has rebelled for most of her life, and college is doing nothing to change that fact. Until one sorority night, when she witnesses the unthinkable and stumbles upon a monster from another realm. A monster who makes her question everything.

Including her desire for the beast.

Perfect for fans of Ice Planet Barbarians, The Spider's Mate, and Beauty and the Beast. Frost Claim is inspired by Krampus and book one in this fantasy romance series with enemies to lovers, plenty of banter, heavy steam, and sexy monsters you won't be able to resist.

FROST CLAIM

Book 1 in the Demons of Frosteria Series

Coming October 2022
Pre-Order Now

ACKNOWLEDGMENTS

We hoped you enjoyed Korreth and Zira's story! A book, no matter the size, is given all our heart, sweat, and tears. And in this case, maybe some snow.

Our first thank you is to our families, who keep us on our toes each day. We would not have been able to do this without Amber H., Jerica, Lou, Ann, Amber D., and Hayley. You guys are truly amazing and helped us really bring this story to life.

A final thank you to our dear readers for entering the start of our brand new series! We wanted to bring something sexy, dark, and with a whole new spin on Krampus and demons. And we can't wait for you to read Aeryx and Noel's story next! Be sure to follow us on social media so you'll be up to date on the latest news in the demon realm!

THE OFFICIAL PLAYLIST

Want to listen along while you read and immerse yourself into the world? Listen to the playlist below!

1. Love Like Winter by AFI
2. Ice Queen by Within Tempation
3. Blodfest by Danheim
4. Blood Tear by J2
5. Seven Nation Army by SKALD
6. Berserkir by Danheim
7. Endlessly by Chevelle
8. Get The Lead Out by A Perfect Circle
9. Snowblind by Cold
10. Monsters by Shinedown

ABOUT ELLE BEAUMONT

 Elle Beaumont loves creating vivid and fantastical worlds. She lives in south-eastern, Massachusetts with her husband and two children. When not writing or chasing around her children, she enjoys making candles. More than once she has proclaimed that coffee is the lifeblood and it is how she refrains from becoming a zombie.

Stay up to date and receive some free books by signing up for her newsletter! ellebeaumontbooks.com/newsletter

Join Elle's Facebook group and hang out with her
facebook.com/groups/ElleBeaumontStreetTeam

For more information visit
www.ellebeaumontbooks.com
Follow Elle on social media!

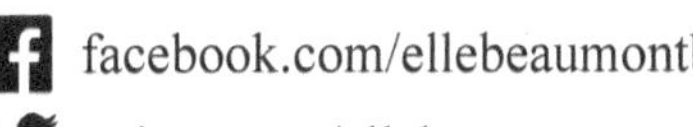 facebook.com/ellebeaumontbooks

twitter.com/ellebeaumont

 instagram.com/ellebeaumontbooks

MORE FROM ELLE

Standalones

Die From A Broken Heart

The Dragon's Bride

The Castle of Thorns

Demons of Frosteria

Frost Mate

Frost Claim (Oct '22)

Immortal Realms Trilogy

Seeds of Sorrow (May '22)

The Hunter Series

Hunter's Truce

Royal's Vow

Assassin's Gambit

Queen's Edge

Secrets of Galathea

Brotherhood of the Sea

Bindings of the Sea

Voice of the Sea

King of the Sea

Anthologies

Of The Deep

Blood From A Stone

Cirque de vol Mystique

Link by Link

Something in the Shadows

Stories for Nerds Vol. 1

Beyond the Cogs

Emporium of Superstition (Oct '22)

ABOUT CANDACE ROBINSON

 Candace Robinson spends her days consumed by words and hoping to one day find her own DeLorean time machine. Her life consists of avoiding migraines, admiring Bonsai trees, watching classic movies, and living with her husband and daughter in Texas—where it can be forty degrees one day and eighty the next.

Stay up to date by signing up for Candace's newsletter! http://eepurl.com/dhV0yv

Join Candace's Facebook group and hang out with her
facebook.com/groups/candacesprettymonsters

Follow Candace on social media!

facebook.com/literarydust

instagram.com/literarydust

MORE FROM CANDACE

Wicked Souls Duology

Vault of Glass

Bride of Glass

Cruel Curses Trilogy

Clouded By Envy

Veiled By Desire

Shadowed By Despair

Cursed Hearts Duology

Lyrics & Curses

Music & Curses

Letters Duology

Dearest Clementine: Dark and Romantic Monstrous Tales

Dearest Dorin: A Romantic Ghostly Tale

Campfire Fantasy Tales

Lullaby of Flames

A Layer Hidden

The Celebration Game

Faeries of Oz Series

Lion

Tin

Crow

Ozma

Tik-Tok

Demons of Frosteria

Frost Mate

Frost Claim (Oct '22)

Vampires in Wonderland

Rav

Maddie

Standalones

Merciless Stars

The Bone Valley

Between the Quiet

Hearts Are Like Balloons

Bacon Pie

Avocado Bliss

MORE BOOKS YOU'LL LOVE

If you enjoyed this story, please consider leaving a review!

Then check out more books from Midnight Tide Publishing!

The Prince's Wing by Amber R. Duell

A ROYAL GUARD. A FORCED REBEL.

Lord Saer Tufaro was raised to be the prince's Wing—the truest and most loyal personal guard a royal could ask for. He would gladly sacrifice his life to save his best friend—the future king of Eradrist—but that may be exactly what the rebels have planned.

The Red Asters were the ones to place Saer in the palace after the old king was usurped. Close to the throne and above suspicion, he was to be an invaluable tool for the cause. But a spy is only useful if his loyalties aren't torn.

When the prince is manipulated into an arranged marriage to the former king's bastard daughter, tension in the palace grows. The Lady is as innocent as she is beautiful and would make the prince a wonderful wife. If only she didn't make Saer's heart race…

Available Now

A Cursed Kiss by Jenny Hickman

Living on an island plagued by magic and mythical monsters isn't a fairy tale... it's a nightmare.

After Keelynn witnesses her sister's murder at the hands of the legendary Gancanagh, an immortal creature who seduces women and kills them with a cursed kiss, she realizes there's nothing she wouldn't do to get her back. With the help of a vengeful witch, she's given everything she needs to resurrect the person she loves most.

But first, she must slay the Gancanagh.

Tadhg, a devilishly handsome half-fae who has no patience for high society—or propriety—would rather spend his time in the company of loose women and dark creatures than help a human kill one of his own.

That is until Keelynn makes him an offer he can't refuse.

Together, they embark on a cross-country curse-breaking mission that promises life but ends in death.

Available Now